KUDOS for *You're As Good As Dead*

"The scary thing about E.A. Aymar is not that he is one of the most promising and talented hard boiled crime writers of his generation, but that he tells his tales of revenge like he has actually lived them." ~ Vincent Zandri, *NY Times* and *USA Today* Bestselling Author of *Everything Burns*, *The Remains*, and *Moonlight Weeps*.

"E. A. Aymar delivers it all—innocence threatened, harrowing suspense, and a terrific pace. *You're as Good as Dead* is a propulsive thriller that drags you under and doesn't let you up for air." ~ Barry Lancet, award-winning author of *Japantown* and *Tokyo Kill*

"Like Aymar's first book, this one is fast-paced, filled with edge-of-your-seat tension, and will keep you turning pages from beginning to end." ~ Taylor Jones, Reviewer

"Aymar has a way with story-telling. Even though our hero is just an average guy, who really isn't very likeable, you can't help rooting for him as he bumbles his way through the complex maze of underworld crime, tiring to keep himself and his daughter safe. And not doing a very good job of it. The book is fast-paced and will hold your interest from the very first page." ~ Regan Murphy, Reviewer

I have to believe they won't kill me, but it's getting harder every minute...

We reach the side and he pulls open the door. I climb in and someone covers my head with a hood.

I'd worn one the last time I'd been in this van.

Someone pushes me to the floor. The door slides shut. Wearing a hood before hasn't prepared me for the experience now. It's stuffy and hot and hard for me to keep my balance when the van turns. I try to steady myself, and a hand on my shoulder makes sure I don't stand. I stay sprawled on the floor, feet and hands planted, and try to keep calm.

I tell myself: They aren't going to kill me. I'd already be dead if they wanted to kill me.

Probably.

It's hard not to think about Diane as we drive in her van. I used to imagine her as a child, picture what her life had been like to create the killer she became. Had she been beaten, molested, raped, arrested? I'd remember her face, large and round with faded blue eyes and giant blonde hair on top, and reverse her age until I saw a small child, a young girl reaching up to hold hands with those who would eventually wound her. But Diane had threatened Julie, so regret never came.

Diane was nothing but a remorseless assassin who had made my life hell. I don't want to think about Diane. I think about Julie instead. They hadn't taken her, which meant that, even if my life is in danger, Julie's safe.

But I'm not in danger.

I won't be killed.

They'd have done it already.

I need to believe that. Otherwise, that fear won't stay sitting in the bottom of my stomach. It'll rise.

Three years have passed since Tom Starks, a Baltimore community college professor and single father, tried to avenge his wife's death by hiring a hit man. Tom is now hopeful that he has left the world of violence and murder behind. But he is drawn back into Baltimore's criminal underground after he witnesses the assassination of an influential crime boss. To make matters worse, it appears the FBI has discovered Tom's involvement and they force him to work with them as an informer. Now Tom must navigate a deadly path between warring crime families and ruthless federal agents, even as he desperately tries to keep his involvement a secret from those closest to him.

ACKNOWLEDGEMENTS

I'm really into thanking people, but I hate writing these acknowledgement sections because I'm always afraid I'll miss someone. Apologies in advance.

Thanks to everyone at Black Opal Books for publishing this trilogy, particularly the tireless Lauri Wellington, L.P., Faith, and Jack.

I owe a lot to my fantastic first readers, who provided invaluable advice and comments: Natalie Ivanov, Michele Greene, Amy Roach, Alan Orloff and Jenny Drummey. And I have to mention my terrific first editor, Alice Peck, who edits everything I write and always will.

I've worked with the same artist for years now, and her work still surprises and impresses me. Angela Del Vecchio, you're the best.

Thanks to Peggy Keegan, for her invaluable marketing advice. And thanks to everyone I work with. Too many to name, but I always have to mention Molly.

Special mention to everyone at the Washington Independent Review of Books. I was a fan of the Independent long before they gave me a monthly column. I love working with that site, both because of the quality of the writing in the other columns and reviews, and because it's given me the chance to work with Holly Smith, a terrific editor and nifty lady.

I'd also like to thank some of the festivals that were nice enough to have me, particularly the Gaithersburg Book

Festival and Fall for the Book. And along those lines, thanks to the incomparable Sara Jones, rising blues star Andy Poxon, and one of the best independent bookstores around, One More Page Books. And much love to Marymount and GMU, especially Dr. Rippy, Bill Miller and Art Taylor.

I've made some cool friends in the mystery and thriller writing worlds and I can't possibly name everyone, but special mention to everyone at ITW, MWA, SinC, Crime Factory, Yellow Mama and Criminal Minds.

And gigantic thanks to my wonderful agent, Michelle Richter (and everyone in the Fuse Literary family) for taking a chance on me. I love working with you, and hope to for years.

As always, thanks to my parents for their constant support. And my lovely wife, who shows me nothing is impossible. And Noah. Kid, you're everything to us.

See you in the next book.

YOU'RE AS GOOD AS DEAD

Book Two in the Dead Trilogy

E. A. Aymar

A Black Opal Books Publication

GENRE: MYSTERY/THRILLER/SUSPENSE/MAINSTREAM

YOU'RE AS GOOD AS DEAD ~ Book Two in the Dead Trilogy
Copyright © 2015 by E. A. Aymar
Cover Design by Angela Del Vecchio
All cover art copyright © 2015
All Rights Reserved
Print ISBN: 978-1-626942-87-5

First Publication: JUNE 2015

Published by Black Opal Books **http://www.blackopalbooks.com**

DEDICATION

To Mom and Dad

and

Mason Aymar (2004-2014)

"And what can I look forward to?
To be hunted and to die. Nothing more."

~ Ernest Hemingway, *For Whom the Bell Tolls*

PART 1

CHAPTER 1

Tom

On a cold afternoon in October, Mack bites down on a potato chip and his forehead explodes.

It's been quiet in Mack's Guns and Gifts until that moment. I'd dropped off my monthly extortion payment while Mack watched the Baltimore Ravens pummel the Atlanta Falcons, a bowl of Doritos near one hand, a gun close to the other. He'd acknowledged me with a grunt and a nod and waved for me to leave my envelope on the counter.

Then I'd heard a loud pop and he'd fallen backward off his stool.

I cautiously walk around the counter and look at Mack's body on the floor. His mouth is open and an uneven hole is ripped into his forehead. His eyes are frozen and intense, as if he's trying to stare through the ceiling. A bloody halo expands underneath him.

"Are you all right?" I ask, rather pointlessly, and nudge him with my shoe. I can admit I'm not exactly a first-responder.

A loud pound on the store window startles me. I turn and lines in the glass are racing away from each other. Someone dressed in black is running toward the store.

And that's when it hits me that Mack's dead, someone killed him, and whoever did it is coming after me.

And I should probably do something.

I rush into the shop's storage room and close and lock the door behind me. The storage room in Mack's Guns and Gifts is small and empty with a second door that leads outside. I'm about to pull open that door and run out, but force myself to stop.

Someone might be waiting on the other side.

I pull out my Glock 30 from the concealed holster at my hip. I've shot this gun at a target range at least once a month for the past three years, but now it feels heavy and foreign in my hand. Still, it's a better choice than my pocket mace. I set the gun down and take out my phone. I dial 9-1 and stop. I can't call the cops. I can't be found here and questioned. If there's one thing I don't need, it's the police poking into my past.

Breathe.

Three years have passed since I've seen any violence, and I've spent that time preparing myself in case I see any more. I've done sit-ups and pushups and jumped rope and sweated on an elliptical. I've dropped from two hundred pounds to a lean one seventy and, for what it's worth, I can do thirty pull-ups in a row.

Unfortunately, pull-ups aren't worth much. I'm not ready for today. Not even close to ready.

I pick up my Glock. My hand tightens around it.

Breathe.

I think about Julie, my fifteen-year old daughter, and my phone makes its way back into my hand. But I can't call her, not with a killer roaming somewhere on the other side of the door.

Breathe.

Mack never told me about any problems or enemies. Of course, a man who runs a criminal network probably keeps that information to himself. I'd stumbled upon Mack's ruthless crew three years ago, when I was searching for revenge against the man who'd killed my wife. But the search had gone down the wrong path. People had been brutally murdered, and I had been lucky not to be one of them.

A man who runs a criminal network.

That thought tugs at me. Mack was in his late seventies. He'd lived a long time working in a dangerous business. He shouldn't have been an easy man to get a jump on.

I hear footsteps in the shop. I hurry to the other door, press my ear against it, and listen. A few steps, then nothing. A few more steps, then nothing. I quietly lift the gun.

I can't hear a thing.

I press my ear closer to the wood.

The door to the shop slams against my head.

I fall back and scramble to my hands and knees. I point the gun at the door. Something slams against it again.

Time to leave. I hurry to my feet, grab the handle of the back door, and yank it open.

A man stands before me.

He wears all black: ski mask, sweater, pants, and gloves. Duct tape connects the sleeves to the gloves and the mask to his sweater, so his skin can't be seen. His eyes and mouth are covered with some sort of tinted material. An empty holster hangs on his side and a rifle is slung across his back. His right hand holds a gun, but it's pointed at the floor.

His other fist turns my head into a strobe light.

CHAPTER 2

Daniel

I stare at the man on the ground and try not to rub my hurt fist. Jesus I want a hard drink or a quick bump or a long ride and the feeling hasn't gone away, not like Vince told me it would when we were in the car, when he saw me shaking, when he said "Trust me, the minute shit goes down, you're going to forget what you need," stepped outside, and closed the car door behind him. But I didn't forget and my mind won't let me, it's like a dirty sink. And I've been punched before but this is the first one I've thrown and my fist hurts, feels like someone's shaken the bones loose.

And in the middle of this spinning circle of pain and need there's Mack's body in the other room and I still can't believe that it's happened, that Vince's bullet has gone right where it was supposed to, that I heard Vince whisper "Geronimo!" into my headset, that Mack is dead.

I hadn't seen it happen because I was out back praying to God nobody showed up, like some kid wandering by because I wouldn't have had a choice and, even though it seemed easier when there was no choice, there's always a choice. But no one showed up and I kept my eye on the back door, waiting to see if whoever else had been inside with Mack tried to come out back, hoping they didn't and Vince killed Mack quick, and everyone would congratulate us, even though I very obviously hadn't done shit. Moments passed but they seemed like minutes, hours, days, weeks, lifetimes as I stood out there, thinking about taking off my hot mask and putting a cigarette in my mouth and sucking the smoke and fire and ash into me, and the knob turned.

I probably should have shot the guy when he opened the door but he stood there for a second, looking at me, and I'll never tell anyone that my nerves crashed so hard I couldn't even lift my gun. We looked at each other, unsure of what to do, and I decked him in the forehead.

He takes a step back. Then another. Then falls.

He's taller than me, probably six feet even, with close-cut brown hair and brown eyes and kind of Spanish-looking and, even though he's not exactly built, he's not fat. He looks athletic but only sort of, like a guy who runs a couple of times a week or jumps rope, even if he's too old to do it, and you'd think he could take a punch but he probably hasn't been punched much. He should have wrestled my gun away and knocked me out cold and jumped over my body and took off into the woods behind Mack's store. In my heart, in my wild beating heart and bright eyes and sweaty chest and wet armpits that's what I want, the decision to be taken out of my hand, to be back home on my ratty couch, smoking myself into another universe and staring at the TV and imagining myself doing this, but not actually doing this.

Vince rushes through the other door, bursts into the little storage room.

I feel hot as shit in this mask, in the whole black outfit, and I know I can't take the risk of being recognized—especially me, the guy working for Mack—but the inside of my clothes are cold with sweat, so much sweat and so cold I wonder if I'm coming down with something. I already have the shakes and a headache piercing my right eye.

Vince walks over and picks up the man's gun.

And then he gives me a long look and I know what he's thinking. He's thinking Dan shouldn't have left this man's gun lying on the floor next to him but, fuck you, Vince, you liar. You told me I wouldn't be distracted once everything went down but things are down and I'm still wanting and craving and trembling, trembling like a car going faster than it should careening out of control.

The guy I punched moans and reaches for where his gun had been, doesn't find it and touches the ground, his knee, his forehead, then pulls himself up and staggers back into the wall and blearily looks at us.

"You with Mack?" Vince asks into my headset and in the shop.

The man doesn't respond and I decide to say something to let Vince know my value. "Answer him," I say. I look at Vince for acknowledgement or approval but he doesn't give me either.

"I was just shopping," the man tells us, and I start to get uneasy because it's one thing to shoot someone working with Mack, another to shoot some guy in here who has nothing to do with this, and my mind is already thinking of excuses, like my gun jammed, but then Vince might make me kill him with my hands.

"What's your name?" Vince asks.

"Tom."

Vince points his gun at Tom's face and Tom flinches hard.

I try not to cringe and don't want to look away or move or anything that would be weak so I close my eyes under the mask's dark eyeshades. "Tom what?"

"Tom Smith."

I wonder if Tom Smith knows he's not leaving here alive.

"I'm going to keep an eye on the front," I announce, and I leave them in the storage room and head into the shop. And there's Mack's body and the air is sucked out of me.

I've seen a couple of bodies since I started with Mack but they were clean, compared to his shattered face and thin bent legs and blood everywhere.

I want to take off this hot fucking mask and go outside and breathe.

I turn off the head set and try not to remember when Mack got me out of juvie six years ago, after my parents left me and no one was going to pick me up. Mack got me out and took me under his wing and taught me shit and gave me a place to stay and food and something as close to love as I'd had.

But not respect.

So I found that with someone else.

I walk around the store after I can't stare at him anymore and look at the dusty camping equipment no one ever buys, the glass case of guns, waiting to hear the final shot. I hear Vince ask Tom Smith something, hear Tom Smith say something, his voice high now, worried. I don't want to listen. I stare at a miniature orange tent, the little ones they put up to show you what the big ones look like, and it's weird to think of Mack gently putting this together, making a little six-inch tent like a man assembling a doll house.

I rub my hands and realize it's been a while since

I've wanted a drug that distraction, and then I think about it and the want is thundering horses.

"How do you know Mack?" Vince asks loudly and suddenly there's a scream.

I look out the window past the cracked glass and into the quiet silent empty street in Towson where Mack planted his store and I try not to be sick, I try not to run out, I try not to—

"Dan!" Vince cries, and all my hesitation is gone and my gun is in my hand and I'm in the storage room and this acrid smell hits me, burns my eyes and fills my nose. I see Vince on the ground and Tom Smith tugging at the back door and I figure Vince has been shot but there's no blood, just that god-awful smell and then I see the small pen of mace on the clean concrete floor.

Everything slows.

How the fuck did a pro like Vince let himself get maced?

I look at Tom Smith and he looks back at me and my gun is heavy in my hand. And everything seems to be happening in slow motion as Tom Smith pulls open the back door and the wall next to him explodes. I look down at my gun, wondering if I lifted it and fired. It's still pointed at the ground. That's where Vince is, and his gun is raised and he shot blindly. Tom Smith and I look at each other one last time and he runs out.

I drop next to Vince and hold my breath from the smell and help him up. He pushes me away.

"Get him!" he screams.

I rush out into the afternoon.

Behind the store there are only two ways Tom Smith could have gone. He could have run around Mack's Guns and Gifts and the closed bridal shop and abandoned pawn shop next to it and into the street, or he could have run into the dense woods fifty feet behind the store.

I choose the woods and, when I'm deep enough inside, I turn and look back at the store and make sure Vince isn't looking out. I hide behind a tree and pull off my mask and suck in air and search in my pockets for a cigarette and find it and drop it.

Tom Smith isn't in these woods but I don't care. I'm starving for air. I touch my sweaty face and sink to the ground and put my back against the tree and close my eyes.

I breathe in the woods.

CHAPTER 3

Tom

Professor Starks?"

I blink back to the present. Twenty Baltimore Community College students from my Wednesday morning composition course are staring at me.

"Are you okay?" someone asks.

I nod and try to gather my thoughts. It's like trying to catch a goldfish with just my thumbs. "Um, what was I talking about?"

The class laughs. "You were telling us what to read next time."

"Right. The next chapter. Read the next chapter."

Students stand and begin to leave. I slump in the chair behind the teacher's desk and wait for the last student to file out, too worried to be embarrassed. When the room is empty, I close my eyes and wrap my hands around the back of my neck.

Two days since the shooting, two days since I'd been lucky enough to mace that man when he glanced away, and escape.

I hid at home yesterday, but returned to work today. Julie's due back tomorrow from a weeklong trip in Philadelphia with her high school drama club. My inclination is to run off with her when she gets back, but I don't have a lot of money saved and it won't be easy to find another teaching job at a community college without a PhD. And Julie's happy here.

More importantly, those two men don't know me.

If they did, someone would have been waiting at my house when I came home from the gun store.

At least they don't know me *yet*. But I'd left my Glock on the floor of the storage room. I have no idea who those men were, or if they have the means to track me down through the gun's serial number, but I don't like to take chances when it comes to criminals.

I lower my forehead to the desk and keep my eyes closed. The cool wood is comforting. It reminds me of a church's hushed chill, even though it's been years since I've stepped into a church.

I have to stay in Baltimore, but I can't hide. And I can't be comfortable until I know Julie and I are safe. The police aren't an option, no matter how worried I am. I'd hired hit men three years ago and ended up killing two people. I'd be arrested if I went to the police and told them my story. I'd lose Julie.

I can try to forget what happened and assume Mack's death means the end of my involvement with his group. After all, everyone I knew in it is dead, and whatever led to Mack's murder had nothing to do with me. But I know I'll spend the next few months worried about the serial number on that Glock, and the rest of my life waiting for the hammer hovering overhead to drop on me and my daughter.

That isn't the answer either.

I have to go deeper. I have to find some way to learn more about those two men, as much as possible, to be sure Julie and I are safe.

Of course, I have no idea how to find them, or even where to start looking. I start to pack up my satchel.

"Professor?"

Two men, both wearing khaki slacks and different colored polo shirts, one blue and the other orange, stand just inside the door of my classroom.

Blue polo closes the door.

Orange polo approaches.

I'm reaching inside my satchel for my spare Glock when the man in the orange polo asks, "Tom Starks?"

"Yes?"

"My name's Garrett. My partner and I want to talk with you."

"About what?" The only way out is the door "not-Garrett" is guarding. The windows behind me are closed and, besides, we're four stories up.

"You knew Thomas Mack?" Garrett asks.

"His name was Thomas?"

Not-Garrett closes the door but stays near it, glancing through the small square window in the middle. Garrett laughs. "So you did know Thomas Mack. Just not well."

I realize my mistake. "Who are you?"

"You didn't know Mack's first name, but you were paying him every month for the past three years?"

"Who are you?" I ask again, my hand on top of my open satchel.

"We're with the FBI," Garrett tells me. He takes out a small black leather wallet and shows me a badge. "We've been watching Thomas Mack for some time now."

Shit.

A shot of worry pours down my throat.

"What do you want from me?" I ask, trying to pretend I'm calm. Does the FBI know what happened three years ago? Do they know about that night at the cabin, all those bodies lying on the ground like dead angels flung to the earth, me staggering toward Diane's old white van with a gun in hand? They could charge me with murder. They could put me in jail.

They could take Julie away.

"You okay, Starks?" Garrett asks. "Or did you just shit your pants?"

He sits on the edge of my desk, a skeletal man with sparse blond hair and a smile that comes and goes like a camera flash and, similarly, leaves you feeling exposed. His partner is short with brown hair, wears glasses, and looks like he just stepped out of the 1950s. Garrett is someone I'll remember; not-Garrett is completely forgettable.

I try to regain control. "What do you want from me?"

"Well, Starks," Garrett drawls, "that depends on what you tell us. Why were you paying Mack? Did his men kill someone for you?"

"No."

"Your wife was murdered, right?"

I take a moment to respond. I always do when that question is asked. I remember just a few years ago, when I was so haunted by her memories that it seemed like my wife's ghost was visiting me, talking to me, lying next to me at night. I remember waking alone, missing her with a terrible longing. Renee was everything to me. Her death left a red wound that never completely healed, and never would. I nod.

"And you started paying Thomas Mack three years ago, right when the man accused of her murder was released from prison. Chris Taylor."

"Yes."

"That a coincidence?"

"No," I admit, careful to make sure I don't inadvertently confess to a crime. "I asked Mack to look into it. He had a couple of guys check out Chris Taylor, and they found out he wasn't involved in her death."

"Renee, right? Your wife's name was Renee?"

"Yeah." Hearing her name sounds strange. I haven't said it in a long time.

"So you've been paying Thomas Mack for three years. For an investigation that probably took a couple of days."

"Doesn't make much sense," not-Garrett puts in from his spot at the door.

"We know Mack," Garrett says. "We know he'd have just killed you."

"I thought of that too," I admit. "I found a way to make sure that didn't happen."

☙☙☙

Days after Mack and I struck a deal for my life, I returned to his shop.

Mack eyed me as I walked in, studying me through eye slits. "You don't pay me till the end of the month," he said.

"I know that. But I need to tell you something."

He inclined his head.

Nervousness tightened my throat. "I typed up everything that happened and gave it to a journalist at the Sun. Your name's all over it. If anything happens to me or Julie, then the story gets reported to the police and published."

Mack rubbed his chin. "I gave you my word. Nothing happens to you or yours, long as you keep paying me."

"Your word isn't enough. Not when it comes to my daughter."

Mack brought his hand down to the counter, set it over the glass case that held a row of handguns.

"You're bullshitting," he said calmly. "You didn't tell anyone anything. You don't even know the right person to tell."

"I guess you have to take that chance."

୧ର୧ର

"I told everything that happened to a journalist," I tell Garrett and his partner. "Told Mack the reporter would go to the cops with the story if anything happened to me or Julie."

The two agents look at each other. "And he believed you?" Garrett asks.

"Nothing happened to me, so I guess Mack didn't want to risk it."

"Who's the journalist?" Garrett's partner asks.

I shake my head. "That stays with me. Sorry."

He starts to say something, but Garrett lifts his hand. "It's okay. Keep that to yourself for now. Because we already know enough. My guess is, we could do some digging and find out exactly what happened back then, and you'd end up in prison for years."

That's true. The thought of getting caught spreads panic through me like jagged branches from a diseased tree.

"What do you know about the Cabin Massacre?" Garrett asks.

"The what massacre?"

"Fifteen bodies. All pros. Two of them Thomas

Mack's people, nicknamed Diane and Bardos, the others from a couple of different outfits. Big fucking murder orgy three years ago, out in rural Maryland."

"I've never heard of it," I say, trying not to change expressions, trying not to let the memories rush back. I'd never known it was called the Cabin Massacre. I didn't even know that night had a name.

"Thomas Mack was a crook," Garrett goes on, "but he wasn't careless. I would have loved nothing more than to drag his geriatric ass into jail and let him rot there, but he was too smart. Now that he's gone, a war is going to break out over his territory."

"Mack had a territory? Like in *West Side Story*?"

Garrett ignores me. "A lot of people are going to try and take his place. And nobody that knew Mack is going to be safe."

"Are you here to warn me?" I pause. "Or arrest me?"

"We're here to use you."

"What?"

"We need someone to tell us what's going on, keep us informed. Mack ran a tight ship." Garrett sounds like he disliked but respected Mack. "Whoever ends up taking over may not feel the same way. We don't want a blood-bath."

"I don't understand what you want me to do."

"You ever heard of an asset?"

"You mean an informer?" I ask. "You want me to find out information about Mack's crew and report back to you?"

"We'll be monitoring you the entire time," Garrett tells me calmly. "We don't want you breaking into homes or cracking safes or whatever else you've seen in movies. That's not how the FBI works. We just want to know a few things about this crew, like who's in charge now that Mack's toast and who else is involved. Stuff we already suspect that we need you to verify. We'll give you a phone with one number. Mine. You use that phone to get in touch with me. Find a good place to stash it."

"No way."

Garrett shrugs. "Then I start digging into your past, maybe find that reporter, maybe some other stuff."

I feel like the U.S. government's heel is squashing me.

"But how do I find them? Mack was the only person I knew."

"Thomas Mack's funeral is in a few days. Go to it. Chances are someone from his network will be there."

"Why can't you go?"

"Our guess is someone else in his crew probably knew who you were. And right now, they're not about to start taking applications for new memberships. We need someone who was already inside. You're the closest we got."

My stomach feels like cold water is pouring into it at the thought of talking to Mack's people. "I don't—I don't want to do this. It's not safe."

"Listen," Garrett says, "this coming war will probably kill you. Someone will eventually realize your connection to Mack. Your other option is we arrest you. Either way, your life is over. And not just yours. Best option, you work with us and stay alive. And we'll help keep Julie safe." That small smile comes and goes.

"But you can't guarantee our safety."

"You're right," Garrett says. "All I can guarantee is that you'll get arrested or killed if you don't work with us."

I look out the window, out to the gray day and the tall dark buildings of Baltimore. A weak sun hangs in the sky, like an aged eye, misted over.

"That's not much of a choice."

"The further you're involved, the fewer choices you have," Garrett says,

"I'm not involved."

He corrects me. "Now you are."

CHAPTER 4

She's wearing nothing, not even jewelry—nude and prettier without it. But she turns away from me and leans over the side of the bed to pick up her underwear. She bridges her hips to pull the underwear up, looks at me, and smiles. "You're distracted," Ruth tells me. "Let's try this some other time."

"Sorry," I lie. "I have class on my mind."

"It's okay."

I stand, pull on my boxers, walk to the window, and peer through the blinds. A small dead tree stands forlornly in the front yard.

"Are you heading home before school?" she asks.

I hate lying to Ruth, but I can't tell her I'm going to a crime boss's funeral. "Yeah, I need to change."

"I thought you were a jeans kind of teacher."

"Figured I'd try the professional look. Why? You want to keep me here longer?"

"That'd be nice. Unless my husband comes home for lunch."

I pull on my shirt, pick up my jeans. "So I'll see you later?"

Ruth laughs and walks to her dresser. Her bedroom is larger than mine, just like everything else in this house. She and her husband Dave live in Homeland, a Baltimore neighborhood I'll never be able to afford, in a house filled with expensive furniture, elaborate antiques, and appliances that are all shiny stainless steel—the benefits Dave enjoys from being a successful attorney.

"Are you going to the shelter today?" I ask Ruth. She works with a number of different charities, everything from drug rehabilitation to feeding the homeless to abandoned animals.

"Around noon."

"What are your plans until then?"

She opens the bedroom door. "I'm going to lie back down and think about you. Or go to Whole Foods. Probably that second thing. No offense."

I look at Ruth and see a touch of sadness in her eyes. There's always sadness in her eyes, even when she smiles, especially when she smiles.

It's odd that Ruth and I weren't attracted to each other when Renee, her sister and my wife, had been alive. All Ruth and I shared back then was a harmless flirtation. Then, a year after Renee's death, when everything was blurry, Ruth and I had slept together once, in a search for solace, and each regretted it.

Ruth stops me as I head out of the bedroom. "I wish you could stay longer but, you know…"

"I know. You don't want to get too obsessed with me."

I kiss her and, despite my distraction, something about the kiss holds me. Ruth slowly leans back into the doorframe. It reminds me of the second time she and I had been together, when this whole thing started nearly a year ago, one afternoon when I'd come over to pick up Julie and Ruth was here alone.

She had been sitting on the steps leading upstairs to the bedrooms, a glass of wine in hand, and waved for me to join her. "Julie called," Ruth told me. "She's running late."

I sat next to her on the stairs.

"How're you doing?" I asked.

"Good," Ruth replied and smiled. "Thanks for keeping me company. Want some wine?"

"Sure." I took the glass from her and drank.

"You don't know a lot about wine, right?" Ruth asked.

"Not really," I confessed. "I don't even know what potato chips would go with this one."

Ruth laughed.

There was something about Ruth's bare legs and arms in her small shorts, tight shirt, and sandals, and in our closeness, attraction stirred in me. I wondered if she sensed it too, as she smiled and laughed and looked at me.

"Dave sort of sucks," she said.

"How much wine have you had?"

She laughed again. "One glass more than I should. But I'm serious. He's a different man than he used to be. We've had some tough times, and he just seems beat down. He used to be like you."

"Me?" I'd never thought Dave and I had anything in common.

"You lost my sister," Ruth paused, and started over. "You lost my sister, but you ended up with this steel inside you. Some weird determination. I used to think of you as a goofy nerd, but lately you've reminded me of what I used to love about him."

"I've also been doing pull-ups," I added, modestly.

"Couldn't tell." She finished her glass. "How come you haven't dated anyone?"

I shook my head. "Haven't looked. Too busy."

"Remember that time in your backyard?" Ruth asked. "In the mud?"

"Pretty romantic, right?"

"It wasn't that bad," she said, looking at her glass, then at me, and then I thought, *When did we start kissing?*

There was a pause as our lips separated, a moment when we tasted the sweet wine from each other. We rushed upstairs and buried ourselves in the bed and each other until a phone call interrupted us. It was Julie, delayed at her school play's rehearsal yet another hour. Ruth hung up and turned back toward me.

Her body was a drug I devoured, and I let it devour me.

But now, a year later, as we kiss in the doorway of her bedroom, Ruth freezes.

Her hands are on my chest, pushing me away.

"Is that the garage door?" she whispers.

I hear it too, something heavy and metallic.

"Probably just a garbage truck," I tell her.

The noise passes.

She nods. "You should get to class."

Ruth follows me downstairs. I pass through her stately living room and then the great hall toward the arched entranceway. I kiss her and leave her at the end of the hall, one of her bare feet anxiously digging into the other. She touches her neck, the slim hollow in her neck, the hollow shallow like a thumb has smoothed it.

"Bye," I call out, and I open the door and step outside.

"Bye."

I close the door behind me.

A psychologist would have argued I was involved

with Ruth because she reminded me of Renee, but the two sisters actually look very different. Renee had been short and curvy and soft, almost a shimmering presence when I remember her. Ruth is skinnier with angular features, a sharp chin and hips that practically point. Both are brunettes, although Renee's hair had been longer, down to the middle of her back. Ruth's barely brushes her shoulders.

Lately I've found myself thinking of Ruth, smiling when I did.

I'd told her that today, earlier in the afternoon.

Ruth had eyed me, kissed me. "This is what it is," she'd said. "That's it. It can't be more than that. Right?"

"Right," I'd lied, and lifted off her shirt.

☙❧☙

Mack's wake is held at Omega Funeral Arrangements on York Road in Towson, a busy street with a slew of small stores and restaurants and gas stations on either side. I arrive just before the wake is scheduled to start, park across the street in front of a church's school, and peer at the entrance through my rearview mirror. But I decide to stay in my truck rather than head inside, just in case I'm not the only person looking for Mack's men.

No one else shows up.

I check my phone to make sure I have the right time and address. I knew it was unlikely that criminals would come to a public gathering, but I expected someone to be here.

I think about Julie while I wait. She'd come home last night and gamely answered a few questions about her school trip to Philadelphia, then zipped out of the house to see her boyfriend. I didn't try to stop her. I wanted to, but knew how much she wanted to see him. I did manage to keep her up late when she got back, asking her questions, listening to her talk. She's turned from a withdrawn child to a chatty teen, but one who still talks to her dad. I know it won't last.

The door to the funeral home finally opens and a slim woman with long dark hair walks out. She must have been inside before I arrived. She walks with her head bowed. I assume it's out of respect then realize she's staring into her phone.

I stay in my truck as she crosses the street and climbs into a silver BMW sedan. Her car starts, pulls out of its space, and heads down York Road.

I follow her.

I'm not sure why I'm following her. There's no reason to suspect this woman has a connection to Mack, and I don't know what I'll do when she gets to where she's going. But I need a lead into Mack's organization and I don't know how to find someone else. She might be the only option I have.

I follow her as she drives past Towson University and its classically-wide brick buildings and stained green clock tower. The stores give way to trees, tall and skeletal, brown and bare. We drive a few more blocks and she turns left onto Stoneleigh, a narrow residential road filled with small houses and side streets. I have to wait for a car to pass before I can turn and, when I do, her silver BMW is gone.

I blink, slow, scan the street. Nothing.

And then I see her car parked on one of the side streets behind me.

My passenger door is yanked open. The woman climbs inside and closes the door.

My Glock is in a bag on the floor, next to her feet.

"Why are you following me?" she asks. "Did you know my father?"

"Mack was your father?"

"Pull over next to those trees."

I do as she says, but leave the engine running. Trees form a thick border on one side of my truck and a small flat house is on the other. It's hard to tell if anyone is watching us through its dark windows.

"I didn't know Mack had a daughter."

"He liked his secrets."

"No kidding. I didn't know much about him."

"No one did."

Mack's daughter isn't unattractive, but she's not beautiful. Her looks are somewhere in the middle, which is where I like to think I can be found. Something is vaguely Greek about her complexion, as if her skin holds light from some Mediterranean land. She's tall for a woman; even sitting, I can tell she's either five-seven or five-eight. And her face is all flawed beauty: deep brown haunted eyes, a nose that's too prominent, thick lips. I place her in her mid-thirties, maybe a year or two older than me.

"My name's Tom, by the way. Tom Starks."

"Moira. So, Tom, how did you know my father?"

"I owed him money. And I was there when he died."

"Really?" Her voice holds no inflection. "So you saw who did it?"

I shake my head. "They were wearing masks."

"How'd you get away?"

"I ran."

"Nobody who worked for my father would ever run."

"I told you that I wasn't really one of his people. I was just paying him."

Moira looks out the passenger window. "I knew he

was going to be killed," she says. "I've known it for
years. Like waiting for someone with cancer to die." She
pauses. "I don't know why it feels like a surprise."

"I didn't know Mack very well," I tell her, "but he
didn't seem like…" I consider how much I should lie,
and decide on a lot, "…an evil man."

Moira turns away from the window and toward me.
No tears, but her eyes are pained. "You're a shitty liar,
Tom Starks. My father's in hell."

We spend a few moments in silence.

"Maybe just Purgatory?" I suggest.

"Jesus Christ," Moira says. "I don't know what I'm
doing here. I don't belong in Baltimore."

"This is Towson."

"Like it matters. Look," Moira tells me, a hard edge
in her voice, "I'm not really interested in talking with
people who worked for my dad. Or owed him money. Or
whatever."

"I get that, but I need help." My tone turns urgent. "I
don't know what to do if the men who killed him come
looking for me. I left my gun there, and I think they can
use it to find me. I need to talk to someone who can help.
And I can't go to the cops."

"Those men were after my dad. They probably had
no idea who you were. Probably just think you're a cus-
tomer." She gives me a sideways glance. "Unless you
told them otherwise."

"I didn't. I didn't say much of anything."

"Then don't worry." Moira opens the door and walks
outside.

I roll down my window. "Please!" I call out. "That's
not good enough. I need to talk to someone."

She keeps walking toward her car.

I push open my door, hurry after Moira, and catch
her arm. "Please," I say again. "It's my daughter. I can't

let anything happen to her." I want to tell Moira about the FBI but, despite my desperation, I don't know her well enough. I can't trust her.

"Then you probably shouldn't have gotten involved in the first place. This business isn't for everybody, especially people with kids." Something bitter stains her voice.

"I know, I just..."

Moira looks at me with those dark eyes. My sentence trails off into nothing. "I can't save you," she says.

CHAPTER 5

I drive home, unhappy about Moira, the FBI, and the whole terrible mess I'm in. I head into Federal Hill and up Light Street, passing shops and streets that lead up hills with trails of row houses on either side, , the shoulders of the city. Federal Hill is a quintessential Baltimore neighborhood and Renee and I had happily lived here with Julie. I still love the neighborhood, but will never be able to distance it from Renee. Her tombstone casts an endless shadow.

I park my truck and close my eyes. I need to think about something other than crime and death. I need to calm down. I breathe deeply, slowly.

But it's hard to ignore the fact that I'm headed to prison or a grave, drifting toward both options like an armless man in a rowboat.

Nightmares have haunted me since I first tangled with Mack and his people. The longing dreams I used to have of Renee have been replaced. I no longer see my ex-wife at night. Now it's the two assassins I've killed, Diane and Robert Bailey, their bodies rising from smoke and fire and walking toward me. Or worse, they're walking toward a screaming Julie. Sometimes the nightmares come three or four nights in a row and I'm exhausted when I wake. I walk through days emptily, knowing I'll return to those dreams at night.

I step out of my truck, slip on my jacket, and head to my home.

The television is on inside the den. I walk in and Julie and her boyfriend Anthony are on the couch, sitting too close together, a blanket covering their laps. They jerk away from each other when I walk into the room.

I ignore them and sit in the armchair next to the couch. I put my head in my hands and rub my forehead.

"Dad?" Julie asks. "Are you okay?"

She's not wearing her glasses because she hates how they make her look, especially in front of Anthony. That was the kind of thing Renee would have done, and it's another similarity Julie shares with her mother that surprises me. Their body types are close: Julie is destined to stop growing at five two, to have chipmunk cheeks and a round face. Her dark hair hangs to her shoulders and her eyes are the lightest shade of brown. Of course, she dresses less conservatively than her mother did. Renee liked loose jeans and sweaters—she was forever cold—but Julie prefers tight pants and tops that are almost always too low-cut. Like everything about her, it's just enough to worry me.

It feels good to rub my forehead. I let my fingers drift over my head and try not to think about why my daughter and her boyfriend have a blanket over their laps.

"I just have a lot on my mind," I tell them.

"Like what, Tom?" Anthony asks.

I bring my hands to my face and peer at Anthony through my fingers. I'd met him at Julie's fifteenth birthday party nearly a year ago, when he was just some polite

kid who talked to me in the kitchen and told me he had an
interest in books. I'd liked him right away. When he had
called me Mister Starks, I cheerfully said it was okay for
him to call me Tom. I'd had no idea he and Julie would
start dating, and that I'd end up seeing Anthony more often than I wanted.

The blanket annoys me too much to ignore. "Why
are your laps covered?" I ask grumpily.

Julie and Anthony glance at each other. "I was cold,"
Julie says, and she tries to change the subject. "Dad, if
something's on your mind, maybe we can help."

They look at each other again, then back at me.

I grunt. That stupid blanket. I hate that my daughter
has a secret life with someone else. Julie and I had been
open with each other over the last few years, but then Anthony came along and changed her. She floats through the
house after she sees him, beaming so intensely she looks
like she might burst.

I remember when she would talk on the phone and
gossip with girlfriends, her body little in a chair, her
brown eyes excited. Julie would tell me what her girlfriends told her when they had finished talking. With Anthony, things stay between them.

At least he's not a bad kid. He's black and skinny
with glasses and a shaved head and, if I have to describe
the characteristics I want in Julie's boyfriend, Anthony
probably has all of them. He's not disrespectful, doesn't
keep Julie out later than she's allowed, plays football on
the junior varsity team, and, as I said, likes to read.

But I still feel sad when she talks about him. Heart-
broken.

I try not to focus on the blanket and fail.

"Okay," I tell them, "come on, take the blanket off.
What are you hiding?"

Anthony looks terrified. Red blossoms in Julie's cheeks. "Dad—" she says, her voice strained.

"It's okay, Tom," Anthony interrupts her. "I'll leave."

"No!" Julie exclaims, her embarrassment turning into anger. "Dad!"

"Anthony, go home."

He nods.

Julie starts to protest, but I stand and stalk out of the room, past the kitchen and up the stairs. I can hear them in the den, talking low and quick, Julie's voice high-pitched in indignation, Anthony's calm and soothing.

I stop by Julie's bedroom, push open the door, and our pet rabbit Bananas bounds forward. He stands on his squat hind legs at the edge of his pen. I reach down and scratch his lop ears. He flattens himself on the floor, his nose moving up and down.

The front door downstairs closes and Julie makes a loud, indignant sound. I sigh, give the rabbit a strawberry-flavored treat, and head down the hall to my bedroom.

CHAPTER 6

Julie

Fuck. I throw the blanket off us. Anthony freaks the fuck out, lets out a little yelp, and starts to stuff himself back into his jeans. I don't fucking care. I hop off the fucking couch, pull my pants over my hips, and button them.

"Who the *fuck* does he think he is?" I hiss.

"It's okay," Anthony says, buttoned and looking a little more confident, even as he peeks down the hall. "I get why he's upset. It's cool."

"It's not cool!" I tell him. "This is my house, too. He can't just come in here and change everything. I was living here before he met my mom and moved in."

"Yeah, okay. But he adopted you. He's still your dad."

I think about my dad's fucking attitude, how he was probably pissed off about something else and took it out on us, and feel my cheeks getting hot.

"Listen," Anthony says, "it would have been a lot worse if he'd come in five minutes later."

I look at Anthony sitting on the couch. "That's true," I admit.

"When's next time?" he asks urgently. "I need to finish."

It's sort of predictable, even though it's like all guys are predictable in this exact same way, but I love how much Anthony wants me. It's fucking cute. "Next time I see you," I tell him.

"The thing is," he says, "I'm looking at your mouth, and, well..." He peers around the corner again.

I love the idea of blowing him just to spite my dad, but I know better. "Next time," I tell him.

I hold his hands and pull him up and he kisses me and, even after everything, his dick is still hard. But I don't want him to get the wrong idea, plus I'm still pissed at my dad, so I kiss Anthony quick and lead him to the door.

We kiss again but I can tell Anthony's nervous because he keeps his eyes open, looking up the stairs.

"Bye," I tell him. "I love you."

"I love you too," Anthony replies. He looks at me wistfully and turns and walks down the porch, heading toward his bus stop.

I watch him and get real sad. I close the door and let my anger come back, let it wash over me like a red wave.

I stomp up the stairs. My dad is sitting on the edge of his bed. I stand in the doorway and glare at him, seething.

"Hi, honey," he says mildly.

"Okay," I tell him, so angry and emotional that my voice comes out all unsteady, "how could you do that to me?"

"I didn't mean to embarrass you."

He seems so sad, and the apology so real, that it's like clouds clear from my eyes. But I'm not done. "Well, you did!"

"I'm sure Anthony was embarrassed too."

"Yeah!"

"He probably felt that way," my dad says, and I can tell he's trying to be all tactful, "because he knew what he was doing was wrong."

"Dad, we weren't doing *anything*."

"I've been your age," he says, and he must realize how old that sounds because he stops talking and his shoulders slump a little.

"*Nothing* was going on."

He nods. "Here's the thing. You're getting to an age where you're going to be curious about stuff like that and—"

"We've had this talk," I interrupt him, because my dad seriously doesn't remember anything. "*And* they had this talk with us in school."

"I know," he says, looking all helpless. "I just want you to feel like you can talk to me."

"I do feel like that," I say. I don't, but whatever. "Anthony doesn't want to have sex until he gets married because he doesn't want to get someone pregnant."

"You've already talked about sex with Anthony?" my dad asks.

Something about his expression is so surprised, so lost, that I feel sorry for him. But something else in me *hates* that he wants to talk about this at all.

"Have you..." my dad trails off as if struggling with the question, "...come close to having sex?"

"No, Dad! Come on."

But he plows forward. "Just remember that disease can be transmitted orally or anally as well as through intercourse."

That's the worst thing I've ever heard. "Can you never say any of those words again?" I ask. "Ever?"

"I could give you a book instead."

"You mean with, like, pictures?"

"Well, no. I was just thinking of a book that talked about the changes in your life. I mean, you can talk to me about anything, but I know it may be uncomfortable."

"I'm pretty uncomfortable right now," I tell him.

"Yeah." We're silent for a few moments. "You've been dating Anthony for six months?"

"Eight months and three weeks."

"Do you love him?"

That softens me and, besides, I'm not as angry anymore. I sit on the edge of the bed. "He's really sweet, and he makes me happy. And he's smart." I pause. "When did you know you loved Mom? Did you know right away?"

I don't look at him because I know how he reacts whenever the subject of Mom comes up, and I hate that sad needy desperate expression.

"I don't know if I loved your mother right away," he tells me. "But it was pretty soon. Maybe a month into dating."

That surprises me. "Really?"

Then Dad starts backtracking, probably because he thinks that if I know he acted all rash and impulsive when he was young I'll be like *fuck it, me too!*

"But remember," he says, "your mom and I were older when we met, and had both been in love before. So we sort of knew what to expect. Not that it was predictable, but we'd had lots of relationships. And experiences. She'd dated a lot, and so had I, and I guess—"

"Dad?"

"Yes?"

"I think I get it." I stand. "Thanks for talking to me,

about Mom and stuff. Just don't embarrass me like that
again."

"No promises."

I start to walk out and he calls to me, "Hon?"

"Yeah?"

"The thing is, love is really special, but the experience of it can be ruined." He pauses. "I mean, I want you
to enjoy what you have with Anthony." He pauses again.
"Just not too much. Make me a promise? If you're doing
something you're not sure about, or you have any questions, talk to me? Please?"

"I will," I lie. "I promise."

I go to my bedroom, take out my phone on the way
there, close the door behind me, and jump on the bed. I
reach down, pick up Bananas, pet him with one hand, and
text with the other.

I send notes to a few friends, telling them how my
dad just embarrassed me beyond all reason, and then a
note to Anthony, asking if he had gotten home okay. I
hate how he never texts back right away, so I worry and
have to send him another, but then I feel all psychotic and
smothering and I don't want to be that girl.

The doorbell rings.

I wonder if Anthony missed his bus and needs my
dad to take him home. I jump off the bed, open my door,
and call out, "Dad? Who is it?"

No answer.

I hurry down the stairs and my dad is already at the
door.

I don't recognize the man standing on our doorstep.
My dad looks down at me. I've seen my dad sad, angry,
and happy, but I've never seen him scared.

CHAPTER 1

Tom

The man with the gun is wearing sunglasses, a black baseball cap pulled low, dark jeans, and a zipped black jacket. But all I pay attention to is the gun.

"Dad?" Julie calls out, somewhere behind me. "Who is it?"

The man cocks his head. The smile stays. "Get rid of her," he says.

I turn to tell her to leave us alone, but my throat thickens when I realize I'm too late. Julie's next to me.

"Hi," she says.

I look back toward the man. The gun is gone, but his hand bulges in his jacket pocket.

"Hey!" he says, animated.

My legs weaken. "Julie," I tell her unsteadily. "This is…"

"Daniel," he says brightly. "I'm one of your dad's students. He's helping some of us with a group project."

It doesn't sound believable to me, especially since I

don't assign group projects, but Julie nods. "Okay." She looks up at me. "I thought it might be Anthony."
I shake my head. I don't trust myself to speak.
"You still want to go to that coffee shop, professor?" Daniel asks. "The one down the street?"
I nod.
Julie's already walking away.
"I'll be back soon," I call to her, my voice hoarse.
"Okay."
I know his gun will be out when I turn around.
It is.

☙☙

"Are we really going to a coffee shop?" I ask hope-fully.
"Nope," Daniel says, as he walks behind me down the dark sidewalk. I didn't register his appearance before, but he's short and slim with blond straggly hair sticking out from under his cap and a sparse beard. "Car's up ahead."
I stop when I see it.
Diane's old van.
I'd recognize it anywhere: chipped white paint; two narrow, deeply tinted windows on either side; a beaten lifelessness.
"Keep walking," Daniel orders me.
We reach the side and he pulls open the door. I climb in and someone covers my head with a hood.
I'd worn one the last time I'd been in this van.
Someone pushes me to the floor. The door slides shut.
The van starts.
"Where are you taking me?" I ask.
No answer, but I didn't expect one.

Wearing a hood before hasn't prepared me for the experience now. It's stuffy and hot and hard for me to keep my balance when the van turns. I try to steady myself, and a hand on my shoulder makes sure I don't stand. I stay sprawled on the floor, feet and hands planted, and try to keep calm.

I tell myself: They aren't going to kill me. I'd already be dead if they wanted to kill me.

Probably.

It's hard not to think about Diane as we drive in her van. I used to imagine her as a child, picture what her life had been like to create the killer she became. Had she been beaten, molested, raped, arrested? I'd remember her face, large and round with faded blue eyes and giant blonde hair on top, and reverse her age until I saw a small child, a young girl reaching up to hold hands with those who would eventually wound her. But Diane had threatened Julie, so regret never came.

Diane was nothing but a remorseless assassin who had made my life hell.

I don't want to think about Diane. I think about Julie instead. They hadn't taken her, which meant that, even if my life is in danger, Julie's safe.

But I'm not in danger.

I won't be killed.

They'd have done it already.

I need to believe that. Otherwise, that fear won't stay sitting in the bottom of my stomach. It'll rise.

❧❧❧

The van stops after what feels like an hour. I hear the side door roughly slide open. The hood is pulled off my head and Daniel stands in front of me, still grinning. All I see behind him is darkness. Whoever had covered my head is already gone.

Icicles are building in my throat. "Is this an intervention?" I ask.

Daniel's grin widens. "I heard you were funny." He grabs my arm and leads me out. "Hope you don't get killed tonight."

He pulls me into a dusty garage that smells like sanded wood, opens a door at the other end, and walks me through a narrow hallway and into a kitchen. A staircase to my left leads down.

"You first," he says.

I slowly descend the wooden steps and enter a nearly pitch-black room. The walls and floor are concrete and the room is cold. I'm pushed to one of the walls and told to stand with my back to it. I blink and try not to think about Julie.

I can't afford any distractions.

"That's him," Daniel says. It's impossible to see anything. "Where do you want him, Carver?"

"Against the wall," a different, deeper voice says. "Shine the light on him."

A bright light flashes on and bores into my face. I look away.

"Starks, right?" the man called Carver asks.

His voice is hard and low and I feel its menace, like an angry serpent winding its way toward me. "Yes."

"I saw in the cameras what happened in the store that day. I know you weren't involved in killing Mack."

"Okay," I say, because I'm not sure how to respond. It hadn't occurred to me that I'd be a suspect.

"But I know you were paying him," Carver continues. "The Judge wants you to know you're going to keep paying. Situation doesn't change."

"Who's the Judge?"

"Judge is the man in charge," Carver says. "Just came to town. He's taking things over. But we need to talk about something else."

"What's that?"

"Your reporter. You still feeding him stories?"

So that's why they brought me here. They can't kill me until they silence me.

"Yeah. I told him about Mack's death and about the two gun men."

"I figured that," Carver replies. "But I also figured there's no reporter. You made the whole thing up, right?"

"No."

Carver steps close to me, so close I can see the outline of his face and the faint line of a scar on his chin.

It takes everything I have not to shrink into the wall.

"If anything happens to me or my daughter," I say, and the sentence starts off as a squeak, "everything I've told the reporter goes live. And he's not going to be the only person talking about it. The police will be poking around."

"So you're saying it's more trouble for us to kill you than it is to keep you alive."

I nod.

I can see Carver's smile, then he steps back out of the light.

"Okay," he says and adds, almost off-handedly, "We know who killed Mack."

"Who?"

"Outfit called the Eastmen. They're moving up from Florida. They want to put a chokehold on Baltimore and stretch their drugs up here."

"Mack sold drugs?"

"Mack had a hand in everything," Carver replies, "so

you get why the Eastmen wanted to take him down. Word is they're not going to stop with Mack. Word is they're going to come after all of us."

"Why are you telling me this?"

"I want to make sure your reporter knows there's someone else involved. I want to do everything I can to make sure the Eastmen get their share of the trouble. You know, in case something happens to you."

I understand the implied threat and I don't like it, but I'm also unarmed and alone and blinded in a basement. *They're not going to kill me.* "I don't want any trouble."

"Then keep doing things like you normally would, and keep a low profile."

But no matter how worried I am, I can't cut off all contact with these people. Not if I want to keep the FBI happy. And I really haven't learned much. A few names and the name of a rival crime organization. That's all.

I swallow my fear and ask, my voice uneven, "What if those men at the store find me? What if they come after me? I left my gun at the store. What if they track me through the serial number?"

Silence for a few moments. "Not sure how that's our problem," Carver says.

I desperately try to think of something that could make me valuable. "But...if I see them, I could tell you. They might find me before you find them."

Silence again, and then Carver grudgingly says, "I'm going to think about that."

The light burning into my eyes flashes off.

"What's going on?" I ask.

"You're going home," Carver says.

Someone pulls me forward. I resist, but whoever it is pats my arm twice. The touch is calming, and I stop fighting.

They're not going to kill me. I'm led up the stairs and

out into the garage. I stumble, turn, and realize it's not a man leading me.

"We need to talk," Moira tells me, her voice low. "Now."

CHAPTER 8

M oira drives us to a coffee shop in a town called
Edgewater and orders a mocha-something with
a hilltop of whipped cream and caramel wind-
ing trails down the sides. It's taken a quick ten minutes to
get here from the house but, given the dark night and my
unfamiliarity with Edgewater, I have no idea where the
house was.

The coffee shop is empty and we're sitting in the farthest booth away from the counter, which is manned by a
bored teen with a neck tattoo of an anchor.

"Who's the Judge?" I ask.

"My questions first," Moira says. "How'd you end
up meeting my father?"

"My wife was murdered six years ago. The guy who
did it, the guy who I thought did it, was released early
from jail. I hired two people who worked for your dad to
kill him."

Moira nods. "And?"

"And it turned out he was innocent. He didn't do it."

"But you paid my father anyway?"

"Things ended up going bad, and the people I hired

ended up dead. I was paying him to make good for their loss."

A wolfish grin crosses Moira's face. "There's no reporter, is there?"

Why does everyone have that reaction?

"Your dad knew better than to question it," I tell her defiantly.

Actually, there's not a reporter.

I'd intended to find one, but the idea of telling my story to a stranger was too risky. What if he decided to publish it or go to the cops? No, I'd decided, a lie could be just as effective as the truth, especially when the lie couldn't be proven.

"Whatever," Moira says dismissively. "The two hit men who died. Their names were Diane and Bardos, right?"

I'm not surprised she knows their names. "Yeah."

"Did you see them die?"

"Yeah."

"My dad was sad about that. There aren't many of them, you know. It affected him."

"It affected me too." Something's changed in Moira's demeanor. She seems relaxed, as if she's confirmed something she suspected.

"Do you still miss her?" Moira asks.

"I don't miss Diane at all."

She smiles. "I meant your wife."

"Renee was always in my thoughts. I guess you could say she kind of plagued me…" I let the sentence drift away.

"You okay?" Moira asks.

"I don't talk about her much anymore." I decide to change the topic. "What did you mean by there aren't many of them?"

"The people who work for my father. Less than ten, probably."

I stare at her. "I thought he had dozens on his payroll."

Moira shakes her head, sips her drink, and slips into silence. She sets the drink down and wipes her mouth with a napkin. "Carver's right. The Eastmen probably do want to expand here. But he left a lot of the story out. The man in charge of the Eastmen is named Wallace. That's his last name, nobody knows his first. He used to work for my father. They had a falling out."

"I could have guessed that last part," I tell her.

Moira takes another drink and sets the cup down. "Six months ago, my father killed Wallace's son."

"*What?*"

Shadows move behind her brown eyes like thieves passing through a dark house. "The kid had a conscience, and he found out what his dad was doing."

"The kid? How old was he?"

"Barely in his twenties. All full of confidence and righteousness. They got into a fight one night and the kid decided to go to the cops. Snitched on his own dad."

"What happened?"

"The cops brought Wallace in for questioning, but couldn't prove anything his kid was saying. Probably figured he was making the whole thing up. But my dad found out what happened."

"Jesus."

Moira nods. "My dad's men went after both Wallace and his son, and Wallace got away. He ran down to Florida and hooked up with this other group. Now he's back."

"Why are you telling me all this? Especially after you blew me off earlier today?"

Moira bats her eyelashes. "Maybe I'm concerned about you."

"That's not it."

The batting stops. "Every window panel in my dad's store was bulletproof, *except* one. My dad was having it replaced. The Eastmen knew that, and they knew when to strike. Someone must have told them."

I remember the spider-webs in the glass racing away from each other. "That's why that second shot didn't go through."

Moira nods. "The one for you."

"I still don't understand why you're telling me this."

"Someone in my dad's group knew about that glass, so I can't trust any of his men."

"But I can't help you. I'm not involved."

"Wars have a way of involving everyone. And when things get bad, and they're going to, I'll need someone I can trust. You will, too."

I tell her she can trust me, and I wonder if this is enough information to make the FBI happy.

CHAPTER 9

The next morning is weirdly typical, not that I'm complaining after being kidnapped the night before. I wake up, make waffles for me and Julie, and see her off to school. Then I try to ignore everything happening in my life and watch *Sports Center*.

But it's impossible to ignore what Moira told me. I'd called Garrett on his special phone after Moira dropped me off last night and relayed what she'd said.

"Good work," Garrett told me.

"Is that everything you need? Are we done?"

A bark of laughter. "Starks, we're just getting started. We won't be done until you know these people better than you know your own mother."

"My mother and I don't talk that often."

He'd hung up.

I switch the channel until I land on a Woody Allen movie. *Manhattan*. The first time I'd seen this movie was during those first years after college when I wanted to be a writer and hadn't learned it wouldn't happen. I'd watched *Manhattan* and the movie felt like everything I ever wanted to say had just been said by someone else, but perfectly. I felt helpless. There was nothing I could add.

I'd shown the movie to Renee—more correctly, I'd tried to show the movie to Renee. She stopped me right after I suggested it:

"I won't watch anything by that man," she had said flatly.

"Why not?"

"Why not?" she said. "Really, Tom? You have to ask?"

"Is it because he married his step-daughter?"

She just looked at me.

"To be fair," I said, "there are a lot of artists who are pretty awful people."

"Right," Renee said, "but that doesn't mean I have to support their work."

"But aren't you worried you'll miss out on something really great?"

"It's a chance I'm willing to take," she said, and she grabbed the remote control. "What are our other choices?"

So much had happened since then that I hadn't thought about Woody Allen, or seen one of his movies, since. Subconsciously, Renee's sentiment stuck with me. I'd ended up distancing myself without realizing it.

I settle back into the couch and decide to lose myself in the movie, disappear into the black and white film and the problems of other people.

And, of course, my phone buzzes.

"Hello?"

"Have you talked with anyone since last night?" Moira asks.

I press the phone close to my ear. "No. Wait, about what?"

"There's a rumor the FBI is looking into things."

I keep my voice calm. It's not easy. "I haven't talked to anyone."

"Make sure you don't. And make sure you stay paranoid. Everyone else is."

She hangs up. I stare forward.

It's time to get Julie.

Time to run.

CHAPTER 10

Switch

L ook," Lucy says, and we watch Teacher Tom run, run, *run* from his house down the sidewalk and get into his truck. His truck pulls away and goes fast down the street.

Lucy pulls out and we drive after him. I can tell she's happy, even if she doesn't look happy. "About time," Lucy says. "Getting sick of the Judge telling us to keep an eye on some teacher." She makes a big frown. "I wonder where he's going."

"I dunno," I say, and I look out the window at the tall pretty buildings, the parked cars, and the funny people...

"Put that somewhere safe," Lucy tells me.

I look down and see that I'm holding my knife. I lean forward and lift up my jeans and put it by my ankle.

"Open the glove box," Lucy says. "Give me the addresses. Where are we heading?"

I give Lucy the list of places Teacher Tom likes to go. Then I look out my window and the buildings and the people are gone and there's water and different people.

Lucy glances at the list. "Shit, looks like he's headed to Whitegate. He's going to get his daughter and skip town."

I put the list back in the glove compartment and close snap the drawer shut.

"I still have no idea," Lucy complains, "why we're watching this guy. There's a war going on, Mack's dead, we have no idea how many people the Eastmen brought up, and we're supposed to watch this nervous nerd? Carver can say whatever he wants, but this can't be the Judge's plan, right?"

I don't say anything. Lucy just keeps talking. I'm watching a silly bird trying to carry bread that's too big for it.

"And then," Lucy complains as we sit stopped at an embarrassed light, "we're not supposed to ask what happens next? Is the Judge going to move up here for good? We haven't gotten any money since Mack was killed. Say what you want, but Mack ran a tight operation. Food, clothes, money, a place to live. We have this war coming, and I need to know you're okay if something happens to me. Sisters stick together, all that shit."

That silly bird gets swarmed by other birds. He drops the bread, yells, and flies away. All the other birds make a crowd around the bread. Then Lucy drives forward and a building gets between us, and I can't see anything anymore.

After a pile of minutes, Lucy swerves to the side of the road and the car stops. "Check it out," Lucy says and I do.

Teacher Tom is running across the street. He gets to the other side, looks everywhere except at us, and starts hurrying to the school.

Lucy sighs, picks up her phone, and touches it.

I watch Teacher Tom stop, reach into his pocket, and pull out his phone.

"What are you doing, Tom?" Lucy says.

Teacher Tom takes a step back and looks everywhere again. I cover my mouth so I won't laugh.

I can hear his voice through the phone. "Who is this?"

"I'm with the Judge," Lucy says, "and I know what you're doing."

Teacher Tom is still looking around but then he stops. "Where are you? You've been following me?"

"Carver asked us to keep an eye on you, figured you'd freak out after last night. You running, Tom?"

"You don't need me," he says. "I'm taking my daughter and we're getting the hell away."

"Can't let you do that." Lucy sounds so, *so* bored. "And you don't want me to have to stop you."

I reach for my knife but Lucy shakes her head so I leave it.

"I'm not afraid," Teacher Tom says. "I've been around your crew before."

"You haven't been around me. And if you go into that school, there's going to be some blood spilled. You understand?"

"I understand," Teacher Tom says. "But it'll be your blood if you fuck with my daughter."

Lucy looks at me and I see pinwheels twirl in her eyes.

"I like your attitude," Lucy says, and her voice is excited and cute. "But here's the thing. You and your daughter aren't in danger. But if you get Julie and try to leave, then both of you will be."

Lucy and I watch Teacher Tom stand statue still.

"I need you to do your normal routine," Lucy tells

him. "Don't let anyone know anything's different. Keep sleeping with your sister-in-law, keep making waffles, that's how you'll keep breathing. You have class in an hour. Go to it."

Teacher Tom keeps standing still and it seems like for a long time. Then he puts the phone in his pocket and walks back to his truck.

Lucy shuts off her phone. "This nerd might be more fun that we thought," she says.

I'm happy my sister is happy!

CHAPTER 11

Tom

I lock the bathroom stall at Baltimore Community College, sit on the closed toilet seat, and consider my options.

The woman on the phone said Julie was safe, but I don't believe that for a second.

On the other hand, everyone seems to think it's a good idea to keep me alive, all thanks to my fictitious reporter. I might be a liability, but I'm a liability with insurance.

Even so, I don't like being watched. I pull out my other phone and text Garrett: *Call me ASAP.*

I wait for a reply that doesn't come. I bite a fingernail in frustration, unlock the stall door, and head to my class.

Most of my classes focus on composition, the basic constructs of an essay, grammar, sentence structure, and everything else a college student needs for English 101, and they're incredibly boring for me and the students. But this class is dedicated to the work of one author, and we're finishing up a study on Hemingway. We'd read *A Farewell to Arms*, *The Old Man and the Sea*, and are just about to start *For Whom the Bell Tolls*.

Regardless, I'd rather be anywhere else, but there's nowhere I can go and nothing I can do. And the woman on the phone told me to follow my normal routine.

I walk into my classroom, five minutes late, and look over the small group of students. There are only eleven in the class. One's missing.

"Does anyone know where Elizabeth is?" I ask.

No one does.

"All right, Ashley," I say to the twenty-nine year old tattooed blonde who always leads the discussions. "Tell us about the beginning of the book."

"So it takes place in the Spanish Civil War, and the main character, Roberto, is, like, lying in grass or something..."

There was a rumor about the FBI...

"Professor?" a kid named Grant asks.

"What?"

"Are you okay?"

"Sure. Why?"

"Because you've just been staring at nothing for, like, a minute."

Laughter from the other students.

"I'm good." I clap my hands together. "Hemingway. *For Whom the Bell Tolls*. Who wants to start?"

"I was just talking about the beginning!" Ashley exclaims. "Are you sure you're okay?"

The door opens and a man steps inside. He looks to be in his late twenties and he's unshaven with a squat build, sunglasses and a thick leather coat. His brown hair is tousled, as if a bird's nest fell and landed upside down on his head. He removes his glasses and looks at me. His brown eyes are bloodshot. "Thomas Starks?" he asks.

The students are silent. I can feel their tension; tension because he called me by my first name even though it's clear we don't know each other.

"Yes?"

"My friend Elizabeth told me to tell you she can't make class," the man says, and he takes a seat in the back of the room. "She's sick."

"What's wrong with her?" a young black student named Kendra asks.

He shrugs. "Flu, mono, I don't know. Anyway, Elizabeth wants me to take notes." He takes a small notepad out of his jacket pocket and flips it open. "My name's Simon."

I wonder if Simon is working for the Judge.

I can ask him to leave; university policy forbids anyone from attending classes other than registered students. Then again, he might insist on staying and I don't need a confrontation. On the other hand, if he leaves, he might skulk around the halls and wait for me.

Better to keep an eye on him.

"Elizabeth's sick?"

Simon nods. "She said you could call her if you wanted."

Or maybe he's being honest. "I'll need your contact information. University regulations."

"Can I give it to you after class?"

"Yes. And you're going to need to read off someone's book. We're about to start *For Whom the Bell Tolls*."

Ashley nearly loses her shit. "I was just talking about it!"

"Yes," I reply, "but you started with the story. I want us to start with the poem. Does anyone want to read it?"

A woman named Nikki, black and middle-aged with

glasses and a paunch, clears her throat and reads John
Dunne's poem:

"No man is an island,
Entire of itself,
Each is a piece of the continent,
A part of the main.
If a clod be washed away by the sea,
Europe is the less.
As well as if a promontory were.
As well as if a manor of thine own
Or of thine friend's were.
Each man's death diminishes me,
For I am involved in mankind.
Therefore, send not to know
For whom the bell tolls,
It tolls for thee."

"All right," I tell the class. "Why is this poem here?
Why did Hemingway use it as the book title?"
Silence as they study the poem.
"It's kind of hard to tell," Ashley says, "without
reading the book."
"If you had to guess."
"The bells are church bells, right?" a woman named
Wendy asks, a small pale blonde with a hint of a southern
accent. "Church bells for someone's death?"
"It's a funeral bell," I explain. "Dunne lived at the
time of the plague in Europe, and people were dropping
everywhere. They sounded the bell when someone died.
So death was a central theme in this poem."
"Well," a kid named Trevor offers, "he also uses an
island as an image. And he lived in Europe, so it must
have felt like just one big dying island, with everyone
stuck on it."

I watch Simon as Trevor speaks. He's sitting next to one of the students, staring into her book. He looks up, matches my gaze, and says, "If you know someone who died, sometimes it feels like you're next."

I take a moment to respond.

"I think there's a more optimistic approach."

"I don't know." Simon looks around the room. "I'm afraid of dying. And I don't think it would make me feel much better if everyone here went with me."

The class laughs.

"New assignment," I announce. "Write down your..." I try to think of something, "thoughts on the poem. Take twenty minutes and hand it in to me."

Pens and papers emerge. I sit behind the desk, let time pass, and try not to stare at Simon.

My secret phone buzzes noisily from inside my satchel. Garrett.

"No checking your phone in class, Professor Starks," someone chides me.

"I'm sorry. Tell you what. Take your assignments home and bring them in next class. You guys can leave a little early."

No one complains. I call Garrett back as the last student leaves.

He answers on the first ring. "Starks."

I stand in a corner of the room, cup my hand over the phone and tell him about the call I received when I'd gone to Julie's school.

I don't tell him that I'd been about to run.

"Do you have any idea," Garrett asks, "who this woman was or how she got your number?"

"No."

"Was she white or black?"

"I'm not sure. I couldn't get a good look at her through the phone."

"Don't be a smartass. You heard her voice, right?"

"Yeah."

"Well, did she sound like—" Garrett pauses, and his voice is deep and scratchy when he speaks, "—this?"

"Is that what you think black women sound like?"

Garrett sighs. "We're getting off track." His voice is back to normal.

"What if the Judge suspects me?"

"Listen, you're scared, but we're the best route for you to go. We can protect you."

"How?" I whisper. "How can you protect Julie? How are you going to keep her safe?"

"Starks," Garrett says, his voice calm. "I know you're worried. You should be. But you can't go back on this. Do you understand that? If you go back, then you go to jail. But I don't want to do that, because you're in a position to help us. Look, no matter what you may have seen on TV or read in a book, the FBI keeps its assets safe. I'll have security placed near you and your daughter if there's any cause to worry, and we'll pull you out as soon as it becomes too dangerous. I promise you. But you need to think about something."

"What's that?"

"If this Judge really does want to kill you, who can protect you better than we can? Where else can you go?"

I bite my lip, grip the phone, turn, and see Simon leaning against the door to the classroom, grinning at me.

I hang up.

"Important phone call?"

"Sort of."

Simon walks toward me and plunges his hand into his pocket. I take a step back into the wall behind me.

"You okay?" He pulls out a business card and presses it into my numb hand.

"You wanted my contact information, right?" he asks. "For the university?"

I look down at the card. Chicken Shack.

"You have a business card for Chicken Shack?"

"I'm assistant manager," he tells me proudly. "You got a business card for your job?"

"No."

"See?" Simon comments, although I don't know what he means. He heads back out of the classroom. "I like this class," he calls over his shoulder. "Might come back. As sick as Elizabeth was, who knows if she'll be able to make it again."

꿍꿍꿍

I drive home, nervously chewing my thumbnail. I try to remember how I'd dealt with the fear three years ago, and I don't remember being this worried.

Night floats down. I pull into a parking spot a block away from my row house and check my phone.

A text from Ruth. *Miss you*

It makes me feel a little better. I lock and leave my truck. Another cold night in Baltimore, the kind of cold that makes you shove your hands into your pockets, hunch your shoulders, walk fast.

I reach my door, unlock it, head toward the den, and call out to Julie.

Julie's not there.

Someone else is.

CHAPTER 12

on't do that," a woman standing by the entrance to the den tells me.

"Don't do what?"

"Reach into your briefcase," someone else says.

I turn. The same woman standing by the door is sprawled on my couch.

Twins.

I don't reach inside the satchel, but I don't take my hand away either. "Who are you two?"

"I'm Lucy," the woman on the couch says, and she swivels to a sitting position. "That's my sister, Switch. The Judge sent us."

"You were the one on the phone."

Lucy nods.

Lucy and her sister are short—maybe five feet even—thin, and black. And bald. Usually a lack of hair draws your attention to someone's face, but both of their faces are unremarkable. Their brown eyes wouldn't be considered big or small, their lips aren't thick or thin, everything is typical. No distinguishing features. They look to be in their early twenties.

"Where's my daughter?" I ask. I know Julie is with Anthony, but want to see if they know.

Switch shrugs. "I dunno." Her voice is a little higher than her sister's and has something childish and uncertain in it.

"We searched the house and didn't see her," Lucy clarifies.

"You searched my house?"

Something catches my attention, a flicker in Switch's eye, a brightening of her smile.

"I need a pill," she announces.

She bends over and rummages through a backpack lying next to the wall. She pulls out a small round bottle, pops the top, shakes out a pill, and claps her hand over her mouth. She swallows and starts saying something low and indecipherable into her hand.

I look at Lucy. She doesn't seem fazed. Even though they're twins, I can immediately tell the sisters apart. Lucy has a somber, controlled bearing, and Switch looks happily dazed.

"What's going on?" I ask. "Why is she taking a pill? What's happening?"

"She needs her pills," Lucy tells me.

Switch keeps muttering. After a minute she stops, puts both hands at her sides, and breathes deeply.

"We're here because the Judge wants to make sure no one talks," Lucy tells me. "But don't worry. We brought our own food."

"Your own food?"

They nod.

"Do you think you're staying with me?"

They keep nodding.

"No way." I make a quick decision. "Julie and I are leaving the city."

The nods simultaneously turn into head shakes. "The Judge won't let you," Lucy says. "Not till he figures out who's talking."

I'm conscious of the phone in my pocket, the square bulge outlined on my thigh. The record of calls and texts made between me and Garrett. I hadn't put it back in my satchel.

"Listen," I say, slowly, "I don't know anything about you or the Eastmen or anyone else. All I could tell anyone is where Mack's shop was located, and how much I was paying him. I'm not as important as you think I am."

"No one thinks you're important," Lucy agrees. "But the Judge wants us to watch you and Julie. And protect the two of you. After all, we don't want anything getting back to your newspaper friend."

I finally understand.

"The Judge wants to keep me safe," I say slowly, "so my journalist doesn't take my story to the cops."

"Right," Lucy says.

Trapped by my own plan.

"The thing is," I tell the twins, still speaking carefully, deliberately, "this is too much for me and my daughter. We need to escape. We need—"

Switch giggles and lifts her shirt. A knife is tucked into her waistband.

"Sorry, roomie," Lucy tells me and smiles. "You're ours. And we're going to be by your side until this is over."

ഒ൭ഒ

"Moira?"

"Tom?" She sounds sleepy. "What's going on?"

I turn on the faucet in the bathroom and speak quietly into the phone. "The Judge sent people here."

Moira's voice loses its sleepiness. "What are you talking about?"

"To keep an eye on me. Two sisters. Lucy and Switch."

"Lucy and Switch? Oh my."

"Who are you, Dorothy? What does *oh my* mean?"

"Did Lucy say why they're there?"

"I told you, the Judge wants to keep an eye on me. I can't get them to leave!"

"Tom, it's okay. I know these women. Lucy is trustworthy."

"She's not the one I'm worried about. As worried about."

"Switch is a little crazy," Moira concedes, "but she's okay. They're both okay."

"How did you just go from *Tom, it's okay* to *a little crazy*? Don't you realize that a little crazy is the opposite of okay?"

Moira laughs. "She has some kind of disorder, disassociative something or other, I'm not sure. She has to take medicine to keep herself in check."

"What?"

"It's not a perfect situation," Moira acknowledges. "But as long as she has her pills, she's okay. Sort of."

"I'm not letting some psychopath stay with me and my daughter!"

"Psychopath is a strong word," Moira chides me, then pauses. "Well, maybe not. Anyway, neither Switch nor Lucy would harm a child, even if the Judge ordered it. I know them. Julie's safe. But if you're worried, send her to stay with someone you know. The Judge said no one can leave the city, so you can't send her out of town. But if you have relatives who can put her up in Baltimore, it might make you feel better."

"Nothing will make me feel better." I pause. "Are you sure the Judge will go for that?"

"I'm sure. And you'll be fine. You're innocent. Stay that way."

Julie pops into the den when she gets home.

"I was at Anthony's," she volunteers. "His mom made me dinner, so I'm not hungry."

"Can you come here for a minute?"

"Sure." Julie walks into the room and curls on the couch, typing on her phone without looking up. I don't even have to ask who she's sending a message to. She's just back from seeing Anthony and I know she's already texting him.

"I need to ask you something."

"This isn't like our last conversation, is it?" Julie asks, still staring down at her phone.

I'm confused for a moment, then I remember our awkward conversation about sex. "Um, no. I need you to stay with your aunt Ruth and Dave for a few days."

"Okay," Julie says, easily enough. She finishes texting and looks up.

I feel like I should explain a bit further. "I have friends coming here. Actually, they're sisters, and they're already here. In the guest room."

Julie's expression and voice turn playful. "Really? Why do I need to stay with Ruth and Dave?"

I test the response Lucy and I rehearsed. "One of them is a former student of mine and getting over a drug addiction, and her sister and I are helping her through it. I don't want you around a bad influence."

"What's she addicted to?"

"Cocaine."

"That poor woman," Julie says. Her eyes are concerned. "Actually, dad, I'd like to stay and help, if that's okay."

The older Julie grows, the less predictable she becomes.

"That's really nice," I tell her. "But I think it's better if she gets some peace and quiet."

Julie scrunches her face. "So you're going to let a drug addict you barely know stay in our house? With her sister?"

"Her sister and I don't want to overwhelm her with too many people around."

Julie nods and, thank God, accepts it. "Okay," she says, yawns, and stands. "I'm tired."

She walks over to me, bends, and hugs me. I feel her thin arms around my neck and I close my eyes, enjoying the moment.

"Dad?" she asks.

"Yes?"

"You can let go now."

"Oh, sorry."

Julie smiles and heads upstairs. I wait a few moments then quietly follow her. I watch her walk into her room. The door closes behind her. I head over to the guest room and knock softly on the door. Lucy lets me in. Switch is sitting on the floor, throwing cards into a pile.

"My daughter's leaving soon," I tell them, looking down at Switch. She tosses a card. "I'm not telling you where. She'll stay in the city to make the Judge happy, but not with us."

"I'll let the Judge know," Lucy says. A pile of clothes are on the bed, a long duffel bag on the floor. "It won't matter. He cares about you, not her."

"And tell the Judge this. I've updated my reporter friend. If anything happens to me or Julie…"

Lucy waves away my words. "We figured you would."

"How long are you two going to be here?"

Lucy unfolds some shirts and put them in separate piles. All of their clothes are black. "I'm not sure."

"A couple of days?"

"I dunno," Switch says.

"I heard there aren't many of you," I tell them. "Less than ten."

Lucy doesn't seem surprised. "And probably less now." She pauses. "Which means the ones still standing are pretty good."

I sense the threat but ignore it. "Are your names really Lucy and Switch?"

"I dunno," Switch says again.

I turn toward Lucy. "Is that all she says?"

Lucy lifts a stack of shirts and looks around. "You don't have a dresser?"

"Not in here."

"I could guess your wife is dead," Lucy remarks. "This house needs a woman."

Everything in me stops. "She was killed."

"I know the story," Lucy tells me. "Doesn't change the fact that you need another dresser."

Switch laughs. My hand aches for my gun.

CHAPTER 13

I wake the next morning with a pain in my chest and a sudden, sickening realization that I've let two assassins spend the night in the same house as me and Julie.

Voices in the kitchen. I hurry downstairs and see Julie and Lucy sitting on stools and laughing. Switch stands on the other side of the counter.

"What's going on?" I ask.

"Switch made pancakes," Julie announces happily. "And they're awesome."

I blink. "What?"

"Pancakes," Lucy says. "Want some?"

"No," I tell her, still shaken.

The sooner I can get Garrett the information he needs, the sooner the FBI can act, and the sooner Lucy and Switch will be gone.

But then what?

Will the Judge be able to find me? Will Julie and I have to enter witness protection?

"Tom," Lucy says. "I want to say thanks for letting me and my sister stay here."

"It won't be for long," I reply.

Julie pouts. "I like having them around. I got up early this morning and they were downstairs watching TV. Dad, you didn't tell me they were twins. That's awesome. We talked for, like, hours. And I want them to meet Anthony. He's *really* funny and super smart and he..."

Julie keeps discussing her favorite subject while I watch Switch. Her body language is different from other women I've observed, even her sister. Women are usually empathetic, one nodding while the other speaks. Switch is distant from Julie, impassive. She's not remote enough to be rude, but her reactions are definitely forced.

And then I realize something more important: the twins are wearing thin shirts and shorts. From what I can tell, neither is carrying a weapon.

And the knife rack is inches from my hand.

"...and Anthony is so smart," Julie is saying. "Even dad says he's smart. Anthony reads all the time, like, *all* the time. But, I mean, he still likes hip hop and stuff."

Of course, I can't kill these two women in front of my daughter. But maybe I can lure Switch into the basement when Julie is out. And then Lucy.

The thought doesn't bother me. Something changed in me the moment the Judge placed his people in my house. Ever since they exposed my daughter to danger.

"I don't really like rap," Lucy says.

"Oh, yeah, me neither," Julie replies, which is a lie. "It's mainly Anthony who listens to it."

Julie keeps talking as I imagine the twins' bodies in my basement. But then what? I can't turn to Garrett. He's made it clear I need a bargaining chip with the FBI.

"All right," Julie finishes, and she hops off her stool. "I need to head to school. How long am I going to be at Ruth's?"

"Just a couple of days," I say.

"Okay."

Julie walks out of the kitchen and I start to doubt I can kill the twins. The desire and willingness are there, but I'm not a trained fighter.

A different idea occurs to me, but it's just the first steps of a plan.

"I want to meet with the Judge," I tell the twins.

My plan is to give the FBI what they want. Right now.

Lucy closes the refrigerator door and turns to me. "No, you don't."

Switch's hand shoots to her mouth and she stifles a giggle.

"I need to make sure the Judge knows I'm trustworthy," I continue. "I know you're here to keep an eye on me, but—"

"No one meets with the Judge," Lucy says. "He comes to you."

"What is he, a tornado?" I ask. "I'm sure you have a way to get in touch with him."

Lucy crosses her arms over her chest. "It's not a good idea."

"Listen," I tell them, and the plan forms, "I have something the Judge needs."

Lucy smiles. "What do you have that he needs?"

"The name of my reporter."

Lucy's smile stays, but her eyes sharpen. "In exchange for what?"

"The freedom to take my daughter away from here. The freedom to be left alone."

I don't trust the Judge to give me that freedom, but it doesn't matter. As soon as the twins agree to set up a meeting with the Judge, I'll call Garrett and have the FBI follow us.

I'll have a small problem coming up with a reporter's name, but I can make someone up and, hopefully, Garrett will show up before the Judge realizes it's a fake. Or I can name an actual reporter. After all, the FBI will arrest the Judge before he acts.

Hopefully.

"All right," Lucy says. "Let's do it."

"Really? When?"

"Now. He'll come here."

This was faster than I'd hoped. Or wanted.

"Right now?"

Lucy nods curtly and heads upstairs. Switch skips out of the room after her. I try to text Garrett's number off my regular phone because I buried the one he gave me under a large stone in my backyard last night, but I can't finish typing by the time I hear the twins returning. I delete what I've written and shove my phone into my pocket.

"I need to talk to Julie," I say, trying to buy enough time to send a message. "I don't want her here when he comes."

"She already left for school." Lucy holds out her hand. "Give me your phone."

"Why?"

She smiles. "The Judge is weird about cameras and recording devices. Go figure."

I hand her my phone.

"Now what?"

"Now we wait," Lucy says. "No one leaves the kitchen until he shows up."

She slips my phone into her pocket and I watch my last chance to text Garrett disappear.

CHAPTER 14

Lucy means it; she and Switch won't leave my side until the Judge shows up. Twenty minutes pass and we're still sitting in the kitchen.

"Can I at least use the bathroom?" I ask.

"Not without one of us standing next to you," Lucy says.

Switch giggles.

"I'll wait."

Under the table, my leg is shaking. I'm trying to stay calm, but my thoughts are swirling. The best I can do is give the Judge a name and hope he leaves. Then I'll tell Garrett whatever I can about the Judge and that information has to be enough. I can't work for him any longer.

I hear a knock on the front door. My leg stops moving, and I try to keep my face impassive. Switch heads out to get him. Lucy and I stay at the kitchen table.

"Are you sure you're ready for this?" Lucy asks me quietly.

"What do you mean?"

Moira walks into the kitchen. Switch trails her.

"You're the Judge?" I ask, confused.

"Nope."

"We figured you should talk to her first," Lucy says.

Truthfully, I'm relieved. The more time I had to think about my plan, the more holes I found in it: the Judge could make me contact the reporter in front of him, or he could kill me once he had the name, or he'd lose patience and kill me without a name.

Most of the flaws in my plan involve me being killed.

"Mind if we talk somewhere private?" Moira asks.

"Sure," I tell her. "Let's head upstairs."

✂✂✂

I close my bedroom door behind us.

"What are you thinking?" Moira asks. "You don't want to meet with the Judge."

"Yeah, I do. No matter what Lucy or her insane sister said."

"Switch is a little off," Moira admits. "But you can trust her. She only does what Lucy tells her."

I'm not reassured.

"Why do you want to meet the Judge?" Moira asks.

"I want to reason with him," I lie. I can't tell Moira the truth. I can't risk her discovering that the FBI is involved.

"The Judge isn't like my father," she says. "He won't negotiate."

"I thought you didn't know much about the Judge."

"I don't, but I didn't tell you everything I know."

"I'm not sure I follow—"

"His name was Freddy," Moira tells me, "and he was one of my dad's men. We dated in secret for about a year then, when I got pregnant, Freddy and I married in private. I told my dad everything after the ceremony."

"I'm guessing Mack took the news well?" I ask.

She gives me a thin smile. "He wasn't happy. Didn't talk to me for a week. I understood why: a secret marriage, pregnancy, one of his men involved."

"So when did he come around?"

"After I lost the baby," Moira says, her voice fraying at the edges. "A month after the wedding."

"I'm sorry."

"Freddy and I were in pain," she tells me, heavily. "He never really recovered. He was already emotional, and this was more than he could handle. So Freddie turned away from me, and I was too hurt to reach out to him. My dad noticed our distance. He asked me about it, yelled at Freddy, none of it helped." Moira touches her hair, tugs it. "One night Freddy came home, drunk, angry and stupid. I was in a pissy mood too, and we got into an argument. He hit me. He never had before, but I kicked him out of the house. I don't put up with that shit. My dad didn't put up with that shit either. He saw me the next day and, even though I tried to hide it with makeup, he knew.

"And then I did something I regret."

Moira's voice is so soft I struggle to hear her. The entire house is silent, as if it's waiting for her to finish.

"What did you do?"

"My dad asked if I wanted him to take care of Freddy. I said yes." She clears her throat. "My father called the Judge, and Freddy didn't come home the next day, or the day after. I asked my dad if he could help find him, but he was just...weird. So I asked one of his men, who had been close with Freddy, and he told me the truth. He told me the Judge had torn his body apart."

"Why are you telling me this?" I ask.

Moira wipes her tears. "You need to know who you're dealing with," she says. "Don't push things with the Judge. You won't survive."

CHAPTER 15

Who's she?"

"That," I tell one of the students in my composition class later that afternoon, "is Lucy. She's studying to be a teacher and sitting in on a couple of my classes."

The students turn and look at Lucy in the back row. Lucy doesn't acknowledge them, just keeps typing into her phone.

"Lucy," I tell her, "one of the rules we have in this class is no texting."

She looks up at me. "Do you have a rule against swearing? Because that's bullshit."

Someone laughs.

"No rules against swearing," I reply. "But you'll need to put your phone away."

Lucy glares at me and drops the phone into her handbag.

I smile, happy to lord something over her. That momentum actually carries over through class, and I don't bore the students or myself with a discussion of commas, colons, and semi-colons. For her part, Lucy ignores us.

She pulls a book out of her bag and reads it, or occasionally walks to the door or window and stares outside.

Class is almost over when I hear the phone Garrett gave me buzzing inside my satchel. I'd cut a small hole in the bottom to hide the phone from the twins. It made me feel like a nerdy James Bond.

I give the class their homework and head out after the students leave. Lucy follows me, but we stop at the door to the men's restroom.

"You're going to follow me inside?" I ask.

"Nope," she says, and she holds out her hand, palm up. "But you're not going in with your phone."

I reach into my pocket, take out my phone and put it in her hand.

"Happy?" I ask, and I open my satchel.

She peers into the satchel then studies the phone I gave her. "I will be after I look through it."

I head into the empty restroom. I walk into one of the stalls, close the door behind me, take Garrett's phone out of my satchel's secret pocket, and call him back.

He answers after the second ring.

"Starks," he says. "Where were you?"

"In class," I whisper, and I get down on my knees and peer under the stall door to make sure Lucy hasn't snuck inside. "Why didn't you call me back last night? I called you six times."

"Five times," Garrett corrects me, "and I didn't see your calls until now. Sometimes it takes a while for missed calls to show up on my phone."

I sit on the toilet seat. "Are you kidding?" I ask, still whispering, but harshly. "You're with the FBI! How do you not have a reliable phone?"

"We don't exactly get the mayonnaise when it comes to the Bureau's budget, Starks," Garrett says drily.

"Do you think mayonnaise is expensive? Why did you say mayonnaise?"

"Look, shut up. What do you have for me?"

I open the door and peer out, paranoid. The restroom is still empty. "I found out more about the Judge," I whisper. "He killed some guy that worked for Mack named Freddy, who was married to Mack's daughter. Mack ordered the kill." I pause. "I don't think Mack's daughter is involved in anything illegal. She's just looking out for me."

"Trust me, Starks. Everyone Mack knew is involved in something illegal. Even your girlfriend, this Moira woman."

"She's not my girlfriend."

"Keep it that way. Got anything else for me?"

"That's it. How much longer until you move in on the Judge?"

"Couple of days. Maybe less."

"You'll let me know, right?" I ask nervously. "Before the shooting starts?"

Garrett hangs up.

I wait a few moments to calm down. Then I gather my satchel, hide the phone inside, and head out.

Lucy is waiting across the hall, reading the same book she'd been absorbed in during class.

"What are you reading?" I ask.

"It's a book called *Her Deadly Catch*," Lucy says. "I borrowed it from a friend."

I glance at the cover. A woman in lingerie is sleeping in bed and a man stands over her, watching. The picture is in the faded style of old pulp novels.

"It's a thriller," Lucy tells me.

"Is it any good?"

She shrugs. "Nah. By the way, someone called for you."

Everything slows and stops.

"Who?"

"Julie's school. They said she went home sick."

"She's home?"

"It's okay," Lucy says. "Switch is with her."

"That's not okay with me."

Lucy smiles. "Want to head home?"

We head out to my truck and back to my row house. She notices my tense silence on the way and interrupts it.

"My sister won't hurt Julie," she tells me, as we rush down I-83. "I can promise you that."

"Yeah? What makes you so confident?"

"She only does what I tell her."

"How can you be so sure?"

"Because that's how it's been for years, ever since I saved her life."

The sentence ends and hangs.

"How'd you save her life?" I ask, after a few moments pass.

"I caught my dad forcing himself on her. I stopped him."

"How?"

"With a hammer."

I don't follow up and we stay silent until we reach Federal Hill. We park a block away from the row house, walk to it, and find Julie inside her bedroom with Switch. Switch is standing behind her, an arm wrapped around my daughter's throat. Julie's face is dark red.

I'm too shocked to move.

"Hey, Dad," Julie croaks. "Switch is teaching me self-defense."

"Why are you here?" I ask. "Why aren't you with Ruth?"

"Switch," Lucy says, and Switch lets her go.

Julie rubs her neck. "I wanted to see how Switch was doing."

"How'd you get here? Why didn't you call me? You should be with Ruth."

"I knew you were in class, so I called Jenny's mom. Her dad gave me a ride. Then I hung out with Switch."

"You don't look sick."

"I was."

We stare at each other. I know Julie isn't sick and want to chastise her, but I'm too stressed. It'll have to wait.

"You're going to school tomorrow," I tell her. "And back to Ruth's now."

Julie pouts. "Can Switch just finish showing me this? Please?"

I'm annoyed but, then again, it's not a bad thing for Julie to learn a self-defense move or two. "Okay"

"Let me show you," Lucy says. "Sometimes Switch forgets how strong she is."

Switch agreeably steps to the side and drops to the floor to bump noses with Bananas. Lucy positions herself behind Julie.

"Turn your head to the side," Lucy instructs her, her arm around my daughter's neck. "Point your chin into my elbow."

Julie does.

"You can breathe better, right?" Lucy asks.

Julie nods.

"Now stomp on my toes and push yourself away from me."

Julie lifts her foot then hesitates.

"Go ahead," Lucy tells her.

Switch giggles.

Julie brings her foot down. Lucy moves hers away just in time.

"Push away," Lucy says, and she lets go as Julie takes two steps forward.

"Now what do I do?" Julie asks. "Run?"

"No," Lucy instructs. "You never turn your back to an attacker. Let him come to you. If you stomped his foot hard enough, he'll be stumbling. Watch. Walk toward me and reach out."

Julie walks toward Lucy, arms straight ahead.

"You need to step toward him," Lucy says, and she steps into Julie's outstretched arms, "and bite him." She touches the side of my daughter's neck. "Right here. Sink your teeth in. But make sure to turn your head, because the blood will—"

"Lesson over," I announce.

"What's wrong?" Lucy asks. Julie looks a little pale.

"Julie, give us a minute?"

"Dad, it's okay."

"Hon. A minute."

"What's wrong?" Lucy asks, after Julie leaves. Switch peers up at me from the floor. Both women look hurt.

"You can't teach my daughter how to eat someone to death."

"I didn't tell her to eat them. Just bite into the jugular. It saved the life of a guy I used to know."

"Yeah, Julie doesn't need to know about that." I lower my voice and glance at the closed door behind me. "She shouldn't know about any of this. Do you honestly think it's all right to teach a teenager how to kill someone?"

Switch picks up Bananas and stands.

Lucy shrugs, her face impassive. "Why wouldn't it be?"

I stare into her cold eyes. "How many people have you killed?" I ask.

Lucy doesn't say anything.

"What about you?" I ask Switch.

"I dunno," she replies.

"What does that mean?"

"I dunno." She looks down at Bananas and strokes his ears.

"I don't want my daughter around you two," I tell them. "Or any of the Judge's men."

"You've said that," Lucy replies nonchalantly. "By the way, there's one less of the Judge's men. Carver's dead."

"What?"

"The Eastmen came to Carver's apartment before he got there, waited for him to walk in."

"Jesus. Are we in danger?"

"No."

Lucy doesn't seem concerned. Switch playfully nibbles Bananas' ear.

"How do you know that?"

"Because no one knows where we are."

Lucy sounds like she's talking about the weather, but I'm not as calm. And I can't wait much longer.

I have to turn to the FBI or disappear. This war is getting closer, like a widening pool of blood.

CHAPTER 16

Daniel

I guess they just left Carver's body on the floor of his apartment because Vince comes walking back with Wallace and they're not wheeling a stretcher or carrying a super-long suitcase or whatever else they could use to bring out Carver. They climb into my car, Vince in the front and Wallace in the back, acting all casual, which makes sense since we're in a residential neighborhood, even though they just blew Carver the fuck into hell.

I start driving. I don't get how they can be so calm about murdering because I'm not calm and I was just sitting here. I didn't have anything to do with Carver getting shotgunned.

A hand touches my shoulder and it belongs to Wallace and I don't turn around.

"Thank you, Daniel," he says. "We couldn't put these bastards into the ground without your help."

So maybe I am a little responsible but it's indirect, not like I'm pulling the trigger myself. All I'm doing is telling them where the Judge's men live and driving them to their houses and, well shit, that does sound pretty responsible.

"It's okay," I say, and then I get even more nervous because I want to ask for something but I don't know how to say it. It's like trying to ask for a promotion but the last time I did that I was sixteen, selling fries, and I didn't get the promotion because I was also pretty fucking high.

"Something on your mind?" Vince asks from the passenger seat.

I look at him. He's got this permanent scowl over his face and they say black don't crack but it's like the frown has etched its lines into his skin. This business ages people no doubt.

"Nothing," I say, heading out of Catonsville and back toward the city.

I don't know exactly where I'm going but I've driven Wallace before and he always does this, sits in the back and, when I need to turn, he'll lean forward and touch my shoulder and point right or left. And I do what Wallace says, would probably even steer the car right into a brick wall, because he has this command quality in him and Mack had it and the Judge has it and Vince wants it but doesn't have and I don't have it or want it. But there is something I want, and I try to clear my throat and that turns into a cough.

When I'm done coughing that sickly smoker cough I've had for a couple of years I say, "Mister Wallace, I came to you because you told me that if I was tired of being a driver I could do more for you. But I'm still just driving around."

Vince looks at me with surprise, like he can't believe I asked that, and his expression makes me nervous. and I'm starting to wonder if maybe I did say something I shouldn't, but Wallace just says from the back his voice all tired resigned, "You're not a killer, Daniel."

No one says anything for a few moments and I start to say, "I know that, sir—"

Wallace interrupts me right after *sir*. "What we're doing now is a lot of killing," he says. "There's more to be done. I told you the truth. You won't be driving forever. But these jobs—they're not for you."

"Oh I know that," I say. "I just wanted to know if there was something else I could do."

"There will be," Wallace says. "After we're done with the Judge's crew, we'll run this little city. And I won't forget what you've done for us."

It sounds a lot like what Mack used to tell me, that I had to work and wait and maybe not do so many drugs and also not flinch so hard when I hear a gunshot, but I just nod. There's something about Wallace I trust and, no matter what Mack did for me all those years, I could never completely trust him.

"Shit," Vince says, "we already got Mack and Carver. After the Judge, who the fuck's left?"

"It's not a matter of leadership," Wallace tells him. "It's a matter of loyalty. Mack's men will never stop fighting for him, or for the memory of him." Something changes in his voice and he clears his throat. "So we need to take them all out."

Vince shrug-nods.

Wallace's hand on my shoulder. "I need you to isolate the twins for me. Can you do that?"

"Okay."

"See what you can do. We're going to hit them tomorrow. You'll need a gun on you, Daniel."

I hadn't brought one today and Wallace noticed.

"Okay."

"If our man can't get the job done, then you have to

do it. You have to become a killer. There won't be any turning back. One of the twins dies tomorrow."

I nod and try to play calm, but it's like a drop of acid is hovering over my eyeball.

"Can't believe how easy it was to take out Carver," Vince says.

"Revenge is always easy," Wallace tells him, "at first."

His hand touches my shoulder and he points and tells me where to go.

CHAPTER 17

Tom

I t'll only be for a couple of days."

"That's how long you're letting a crack addict stay with you?" Dave asks.

"It's coke, actually."

I've avoided Dave since his wife and I started sleeping together and I haven't realized how much he's changed. He's a tall former boxer who's powerfully built, but the past year has put some weight on him. His face is heavier, and the biceps he used to be so proud of have turned flabby. He's nearing forty and the changes might be age, but my guilt convinces me it's the distance between him and Ruth.

Dave notices a change in me too. "You lost weight, Starks? You working out?"

"A little bit. Not really. I guess not. No."

"Ruth said you were taking better care of yourself."

I can't tell if there's anything accusatory in Dave's tone. He never liked me, even when Renee was alive. I asked Renee about it once, and she had told me that was just Dave. She may have been right. I've rarely seen him happy. He's one of those men who always seems like something is bothering him, something that would only upset him to talk about it further.

"Is Ruth here?" I ask.

"She ran to the store. Back to the point. Do you really think this is a good idea? Leaving a drug addict in your house?"

"Well, *good* is a strong adjective—"

"It's really not." He squints over my shoulder and frowns. "Is that her in your truck?"

"Figured I should bring her with me."

Dave looks at me skeptically.

"How are you feeling?" I ask, to change the subject. "Ruth said you were sick."

He frowns. "When did she tell you that?"

"When I called about Julie staying here."

"Twenty-four hour flu. I'll be fine tomorrow. Anything else you want, Tom?"

Everything he says to me sounds like a threat.

"I think I'm good."

"Want to say goodbye to Julie?"

I desperately want to say goodbye to her again, and I never want to say goodbye to her again.

But I shake my head. I can't let myself get distracted from what I have to do. Seeing Julie will soften me. "Give me a call if you need anything?"

Dave closes the door.

I head to my truck, climb inside, sit on the cold vinyl and rub my hands. Switch plays with the air vents, closing and re-opening the one closest to her.

I've already killed two people, both at the Cabin Massacre, and don't regret their deaths. They had to die, otherwise Julie and I would have been killed.

Now there have to be two more.

I start the truck and drive out of Homeland.

Switch stays silent. I don't know what's going through her mind, but all I can think about is what I have to do. She and her sister are as big a threat as Diane and Bardos were. Maybe even bigger. They work for the Judge, and something about the Judge scares me, almost to the point of panic. What had Moira said? *You won't survive.*

It doesn't help that the twins are watching me, waiting to learn my secrets.

"You mind if we stop somewhere?" I ask.

Switch doesn't look away from the air vent. "Okay."

I drive north, head to Falls Road, turn on Hillside, and pass through a heavily wooded area. I pull to a stop near a small fruit and vegetable store Renee used to frequent.

"Why we here?" Switch asks suspiciously.

I'm not going to tell her that this small forest is where Renee was murdered.

"I want to walk around," I say. "Collect my thoughts."

"Stay where I can see you," Switch warns me, but then she discovers the visor and, with an excited yelp, bats it and back and forth.

I open my door and step out into the cold. Faint sunlight filters down onto dead leaves.

I can never remember my first kiss with Renee. It happened fast, close to when we first met, the way everything happens fast in a good relationship.

Everything was rushed, happily breathlessly rushed, and the sensations from those first weeks and months remain.

So I can't remember our first kiss but, if I think about it, I can feel that slight touch of her lips against mine, the way a distant sound stirs you from sleep, restlessly stays with you through the night.

I walk through the woods, the occasional distant rush of a car passing somewhere behind me.

I remember Renee wearing a black silk robe I'd bought her, leaving the silk parted, like open curtains, to show her breasts and her dark crowns of nipples, and lower, her rose of black hair. The silk sashes were lazy loops, the kind of knot that drops at a touch, that forms the bow of some suggestive present. One of Renee's hands paused over the center of the bow. She smiled.

I press through trees and emerge into a small clearing. I can still see my truck and Switch sitting inside.

And I've never been here before, but I know this is where it happened.

Renee's arm hurt from where it had been grabbed and she couldn't breathe, couldn't breathe as she ran. She bumped a tree and it tore at her side. Her foot caught and twisted, and she fell. He emerged from between two trees, a long bat hanging low.

My hands touch something cold. The dirt beneath me. The dirt around me. I'm on my hands and knees.

Even now, six years after her death, Renee shakes me.

Years have passed since I've been this close to her, since Renee's memory has been almost physical, since I vividly imagined visits from her ghost. I crawl to the spot where she had lain and touch the ground, feel her warmth in the earth, feel it disappear.

Someone's hands are under me, pulling me up.

Switch.

"Are you looking for earthworms?" she asks.

"What?"

"Earthworms!" Switch says, urgently.

"No. I just, I just slipped."

"Come back when you're ready." She walks back to the truck.

I stay and look around the clearing, at the weak sun, the silent trees, the dead leaves.

CHAPTER 18

"Tom?" Ruth sounds rushed.

"Are you out of breath?" I ask.

The twins are downstairs and I don't think they'll care that I'm talking to Ruth, but I still figure it's best if they don't know.

My voice stays low as I sit in a corner of my bedroom.

"I'm walking to my car," Ruth tells me. "Had to return some clothes."

"I was just at your place."

"I know," she says matter-of-factly. "Dave called."

"He was kind of irritated when I saw him."

"That's Dave. Why is some woman staying with you?"

I close my eyes. "I'm giving her a place to stay until she's better. She's an addict."

"And how do you know her?"

"She was a student. It's actually two women. Her sister is with me too." I pause. "Just for a couple of days."

"Hmm."

My eyes open. I hadn't thought that Ruth would become jealous. "It's not like that," I tell her. "Trust me. I don't want anything to do with her."

"I didn't say you did. I just wanted to know why you're letting a drug-addicted stranger stay with you."

I really don't want to talk about the twins. I open the nightstand as Ruth is talking and pull out my Glock.

A gun shot is going to be loud, and it won't just be one shot. Two at a minimum, probably more. The neighbors will hear. So will people walking by on the street.

I pick up a pillow and fold it over the gun. Then I set the pillow down. "Can I tell you something?" I ask Ruth.

"Okay."

"I don't want to lose you." I keep the phone tucked between my ear and shoulder and press my hands against my face.

"Tom," Ruth begins, and her tone softens. "I don't want to lose you either."

"This can't go on, can it?" I ask, unsure of what I'm saying. "What we're doing is destined to fail."

"I know," Ruth says ruefully. "We picked a path with a dead end."

It reminds me of something Ruth said once before. Two years ago, her parents had been killed in a car accident. The loss devastated Ruth.

'*You married into the wrong family,*' she had told me. '*It's like we're all destined for tragedy.*'

"I was thinking about us earlier today," Ruth is saying as I pull myself up off the floor and head into my bathroom, "and there's no happy ending. The only way this ends is with someone getting hurt. And I don't want to hurt Dave." A hitch catches her voice. "He's been a good husband."

I don't disagree, but I'm not about to sing Dave's praises. "So what happens?" I ask. I take a towel and walk back into my bedroom.

She hesitates. "I don't know."

"We keep going forward until we figure something out?" I hold the phone between my ear and shoulder and wrap the towel around the gun.

"I like that better than the alternative."

"Me too." I wonder if there's any chance of the towel hindering bullets. "Sounds like things are quieter on your end."

"I'm inside my car. Now people are walking by and watching me cry." She laughs a little.

"You're crying?"

"At least every other day."

I set the wrapped gun down and sit on the bed. "You cry that much?"

"This is *a lot* to deal with."

"I guess." I can't remember the last time I cried. Around Renee's death, six years ago.

Has it really been that long?

"Anyway," Ruth says, "I need to get going. I think people are starting to freak out."

"Okay."

"Tom, do you really think it's a good idea to let a coke addict stay in your home?"

"*Good* is a strong adjective."

"It's really not. I'll text you."

She hangs up.

CHAPTER 19

Switch

I am really happy watching *The Voice*. Lucy doesn't like the show but I'm happy she's watching it with me.

I hear Teacher Tom lumbering down the stairs and Lucy's hand with the gun moves under the blanket. I bring my leg up with the knife and rest my chin on my knee.

Lucy looks at me quickly and I remember what she said earlier:

'*He's taking Julie to stay with her aunt. He's clearing the house. Be on guard.*' Then she had squinted at me. '*Are you listening?*'

'*I dunno.*'

'*Good.*'

Teacher Tom walks into the room and it's hard not to watch the TV, so I figure Lucy will watch him and I watch the show and a fat white lady screams out a song. Teacher Tom stands with his back to the wall and looks all awkward and uncomfortable.

Lucy looks at him, just real quick, and I know she saw it too. Everything but my mouth giggles.

"Are you going to use that gun behind your back?" Lucy asks, and turns back toward the fat white lady.

I glance back at Tom and I can tell he's trying not to change his face, like the time Lucy made us lasagna and I tried to look happy as I ate it, even though it tasted like a piece of cardboard someone pulled out of the garbage and that a dog had thrown up on. But I didn't want to hurt her feelings.

"I just have it with me for safety," Teacher Tom says.

Lucy's foot comes out of the blanket and drops on the floor, that way there's nothing blocking her gun. "I thought maybe you were planning to kill us and run off with Julie," she says. "That's why you wanted her out of the house."

Teacher Tom is still trying to keep his face the same, but you can tell by his stomach that he's breathing hard.

"No," he tells us. "Not at all."

"Okay," Lucy says. I guess she believes him. Or doesn't, but she isn't going to shoot him until he tries to shoot her. And that's not a good idea for Teacher Tom.

Fat white lady screams her way to the next round.

I want to dance.

CHAPTER 20

Tom

It's clear that the twins are ready if I try anything, and I didn't help myself by coming down here without much of a plan. So I drop my idea to kill them tonight and, truthfully, it's not hard to do. My resolve had slipped away with each step downstairs.

"Are you from Baltimore?" I ask, to change the subject, relax the tension.

"No. You?"

"Yeah. Born in Dundalk."

"DC," Lucy tells me.

"How'd you get hooked up with the Judge?"

"Mack found us when we were running the streets."

"Were you close to him?"

She pauses. "A little, yeah."

"I don't understand it," I tell her. "I don't know why any of you worked for him."

"Mack found us young," she says. "Most of us didn't have anything, no families, nothing. He took us in, took care of us."

"He made you kill for him."

"Most of us would have ended up killing for someone else."

"But he used you."

"He paid us."

"And you don't think it went beyond that?" I ask. "The way Mack found you when you were just kids?"

"He paid us, fed us, gave us a place to stay. What's your point?"

"My point is I think he brainwashed you," I tell her. "I think he purposefully confused a job and love and all of you would have done anything for him. No questions asked."

"No," Lucy says. "I would never hurt a child. He never asked me to, but I wouldn't."

"Really?"

Lucy looks back at me, her expression vexed. "You're the one who put his own daughter in danger. I never would have taken that chance with Julie."

I start to speak, then stop.

A few moments pass.

"I'll be back," I tell them.

I walk out of the den and head back upstairs. I don't know how Lucy knew what I was planning, but our conversation worries me. Maybe she knows the truth, maybe she's just guessing, maybe I'm acting more suspicious than I realized. I check my gun, make sure it's loaded, and think again about what I want to do.

I know she probably has a weapon on her, and I can't beat her to the punch.

I have the emotions to do it. Just not the skill. Or the element of surprise.

Not going to happen.

I put my gun back in the nightstand and wonder

about something else. Despite their danger, I don't want to kill Lucy and Switch. They haven't threatened or hurt me, and I almost believe Lucy when she says she'd never hurt Julie. After all, she's right. I was the one who brought Julie into this situation.

I head down the hall and, as I pass Julie's room, Bananas hops to the front of his pen and stands on his little hind legs. I pick him up and walk downstairs.

And then, when I reach the den, I see something that stops me cold.

Switch is dancing.

A country singer is singing an upbeat song on TV. Switch's back is to me and her hands are in the air. Her hips shake and her head tosses and she's just awful. She looks like someone receiving electroshock therapy. Lucy slouches on the couch, ignoring her.

Switch turns, sees me, and stops.

Lucy looks back at me. "Thought you were upstairs," she says.

"I came back down."

Switch flounces on the couch. "Shut up and let me see that rabbit." But she pronounces the "r" in *rabbit* with a "w," the way a child would.

I walk over to the couch, sit on the opposite end, and set Bananas next to her. "Don't, um, kill him."

Switch glances at me with an annoyed expression, then slips off the couch and kneels on the floor. "Hiya, wabbit," she says.

Bananas leans forward and presses his nose against hers, his nose twitching excitedly the entirely time. He turns, hops to the back of the couch, and turns again to face her at a distance.

"He's so cute!" Switch marvels. She reaches out and strokes Bananas' ears. "I had one when I was little."

"In DC?"

"We moved around too much to have pets when we were younger," Lucy says. "But they had a rabbit in one of the houses we stayed in, and Switch used to pet it all night. They even let it sleep in our room."

"What happened?"

"We moved," Lucy tells me. "We were always moving."

"Who's we?"

"Our mom died when we were little, so it was just my dad and us. Until we left him."

"So it's just you two? No other family?"

"None," Lucy confirms. "What about you?"

I'm pretty sure this is something she already knows, but I answer anyway. "My dad died a while ago. Mom lives out of state. No siblings."

"I could tell you were an only child."

"How?"

"I heard the story about your wife, about how you tried to get revenge. That's an only child move."

I feel a little defensive, the way I do whenever anyone brings up Renee. "What does being an only child have to do with anything?"

"It's clingy."

I frown and try to think of something else to talk about. Only one question comes to mind. "How many people have you killed?"

"You only count things like that for the wrong reasons." She stands and carries the blanket with her. "We're going to bed. Night."

Switch obediently follows her sister out.

I stay downstairs, stare at the television, and think about what Lucy said. I wonder about the reasons we remember the dead.

CHAPTER 21

Switch

I walk around Teacher Tom's house and make sure no one played with the doors or opened the windows. Me and Lucy do this check every hour, but now she's downstairs eating a healthy breakfast.

I go back to my room and rub a wet washcloth all over me. I don't take showers because Lucy says it's easy to kill someone in a shower. After I scrub my body, I dress and sharpen the long knife Lucy gave me. Lucy likes guns but I like knives more than guns.

I hear Teacher Tom getting ready. He walks heavy in the morning. I listen to him clump around as I sharpen my blade and stay in my room and stare at the wall.

Teacher Tom and Lucy leave. I watch them through the window. Teacher Tom walks to his truck, opens the front door, hits himself in the head with it, and he and Lucy drive off.

I walk into Teacher Tom's bedroom, lock the door, and get naked.

I pull on a pair of his slacks and one of his shirts and

pick up a book on his nightstand. "Hi, class!" I say as I strut around his room. "I teach books. Here's a story by a dead guy. I don't teach a marketable skill. Blah blah blah."

That lasts about forty-five minutes until I collapse on the bed in laughter. It feels good to laugh. People get weird when I laugh around them, I think, because I don't know when to stop. But Lucy doesn't say nothing.

It's not easy being a parrot.

I take off Teacher Tom's clothes and hang them like he had them then straighten the covers on his bed. I get on my hands and knees and brush out the scuffmarks my feet left on the carpet so Lucy won't yell at me. When the room looks okay, I get dressed in my own clothes, walk on the edges of the carpet, unlock the door, and let myself out.

Then I stop by Little Girl Julie's room.

I *love* Little Girl Julie's room! I sit happily on her bed and draw my knees to my chest and fall backward, smiling so hard I think my lips will crack apart. I close my eyes on her soft, white and pink comforter and lie there, knees pressed on my chest, fingers locked.

I sit up after a while and check the time and I have a half-hour before I have to go. That gives me enough time to dance in front of the mirror with a hairbrush, but I only dance for a few minutes.

I think about trying on her makeup, but I did that the day before and it was too hard to make sure that the little bottles were put back in the right place.

Also my red lipstick had gone all the way to my ear. I'd wiped it off. Lucy hadn't seen it but she had looked at me funny.

Then I see Wabbit Bananas.

I pick him up and place him on the bed.

"Hi, wabbit!" I shriek and touch my nose to his. "Hi-ya, wascally wabbit."

Wabbit Bananas leans forward and tickles me with his whiskers, then he sneezes on me. I sneeze back and kiss his bouncy nose.

My phone rings.

Driver Daniel wants me to meet him in five minutes. I dunno why.

I put Wabbit Bananas back in his pen and reach into my pocket and take out a white pill and swallow it. I stand in front of Little Girl Julie's mirror, ball my hands into fists, and squeeze them. I lean in closely and stare at my eyes until the shaking and the excitement quiet and my eyes are just dark dry paint.

"I am calm," I say and, at first, I have to fight down a giggle, but I repeat the words over and over, watching my eyes to make sure they don't change. "I am calm, I am calm, I am calm, I am calm." When my second alarm goes off, I leave Little Girl Julie's room and head out of the house to see what Driver Daniel wants.

ະຕະ

A boring car is waiting for me at the corner. I climb into the passenger seat and we drive off.

"Where's your sister?" Driver Daniel asks.

"I dunno."

He doesn't say anything, then he does. "Thanks for meeting me."

I try to remember if there's something I've forgotten to do and *that's* when I remember my gun is at Teacher Tom's house.

I also remember I don't know why I'm here.

"Where are we going?"

Driver Daniel nervous-shrugs. "Not sure. We're supposed to meet the Judge. All I do is drive."

We pass big houses and then smaller houses.

"Where are we going?" I ask again.

Driver Daniel drives into a little alley with high buildings on both sides with bricks instead of windows or doors. Another car is at the other end.

I hear something and turn around. A truck has turned into the alley and is heading right at us.

I put my hands over my face. The truck smashes into our back and I feel like I'm flying. I hear metal screaming and a cry from Driver Daniel. Then there's a back-snapping jolt and the car stops.

My hands drop and I look through the windshield. The back of the car is crumpled paper.

I make sure Driver Daniel is okay. He has his gun out and is holding it and shaking. I take it from him.

I snap off my seatbelt, push open the door, and step out. The passenger side mirror blows up, and I see a man in the truck aiming a gun at me through his window. I lift Driver Daniel's gun. Truck Man pulls his hand inside and ducks.

I run to the truck and hide under the door, trying not to laugh. After a moment, Truck Man's hand and the gun peek out. I grab his wrist and pull it down. He cries out and the gun falls on my head.

I kick it away, pull open the door, and a boot nearly kicks me in the chin. I stumble back and aim at him.

Truck Man looks at me and reaches for the other door. I drop the gun and take out my knife and climb inside.

When it's over, I walk back to the car. We only have a few minutes before sirens come. Driver Daniel stands in the street, arms at his sides.

I take off my bloody shirt and turn it inside out to hide the blood.

"Who was that guy?" Driver Daniel asks. "Inside the truck?"

"I dunno."

"Jesus. Why do you have blood on your teeth?"

I wipe my mouth. Driver Daniel looks at me and I look back.

The street is deserted, but it won't stay that way for long. Not after the crash.

So Driver Daniel and I hurry away. I throw Driver Daniel's gun into a sewer vent. The little houses across from us don't have anybody in their doors or windows. I grab Driver Daniel's arm and pull him to a busier street.

"I need to stop," Driver Daniel tells me. "I'm having trouble breathing."

"Okay."

I lead us to a building. He leans against it and puts his hands on his knees. Then he bends over and throws up colors.

A couple of people are around. No one says nothing.

I watch Driver Daniel and wonder if I should slit his throat and stuff him into the sewer vent.

I know that everyone who acts a little guilty at first acts a lot guilty later. But I remember what Lucy told me: Don't kill anyone on our team anymore without getting permission from her or the Judge or Scary Carver.

Driver Daniel looks up at me.

"What's behind your back?" he asks.

I let go of my knife handle and let my shirt fall back over it. "The city."

He straightens up. "Okay."

"The city's behind my back," I explain, and the joke makes a giggle rise to my throat.

I am calm, I am calm, I am calm, I am calm, I am

calm, I am calm, I am calm, I am calm, I am clam. I should take another pill, but I get really sleepy when I take two.

I am calm.

"Yeah, I got it," Driver Daniel says. "Let's go."

But we walk a little bit and he needs to stop again, so we sit on a bench.

"You won't tell them I threw up, will you, Switch?" Driver Daniel asks.

"No." I scratch my arm. Now that I'm calm, something doesn't make sense. "How'd Truck Man know we were there?"

"Who?" Driver Daniel shakes his head.

"He followed you."

"It wasn't me," Driver Daniel insists. "I made sure of it."

Driver Daniel goes quiet. Me too.

I'm glad Teacher Tom took Little Girl Julie somewhere else. Because if Truck Man had followed me and Driver Daniel and somehow I missed him...

What's it mean? It makes me squint to think this hard.

Then I realize it means the Eastmen know where Teacher Tom's house is.

I giggle.

CHAPTER 22

Tom

S o," I ask the class, "what do you think of the women in this book?"

"Maria and Pilar?" a quiet black student named Chris asks.

"Right."

"They're okay," Ashley answers, her hands absent-mindedly stroking her long blonde hair.

Lucy is reading her book in the back of the room.

"Maria's the hot one, right?" Simon asks.

Some of the students laugh a little. This is the kind of answer I've grown used to Simon giving—somewhat offensive, hopefully humorous, ultimately pointless. I should probably kick him out of class, but I don't really care that he comes.

I don't suspect him of working with the Judge or Wallace anymore. For one thing, I received a note from the school that explained Elizabeth had been forced to drop out due to Lyme Disease. But, more importantly, there's a difference I can sense between him and Lucy,

Switch, Diane, Bardos, or any of the other criminals I've met.

There's something cold and detached in them that Simon doesn't have. He's too innocent.

"I don't like them," one of my most outspoken students, Kendra, says flatly. "They're poor excuses for women."

"Well," I reply, "that's a fair point. Hemingway's often been criticized for his portrayals of women—"

"It's not just Hemingway," Kendra argues. "Male writers always do this. They always put women in their stories. And the way they make them strong is to make them act like men."

"So you don't think," Simon counters, "that women fight in wars? That that wouldn't happen?"

"I'm not saying it doesn't happen. I'm just saying that the two women in this book are either a victim or manly. And you see this shit all the time, especially from male writers." Kendra looks around the room. "All the time."

I try not to stare at Lucy, although I'm pretty sure she's not paying attention, anyway. "Some women *are* like that, though."

Usually a professor's interjection settles a debate, but Kendra's not ready to quit.

"Yeah, okay, there are exceptions," she says. "I'm not saying that. But they're exceptions. Mainly, the way to act in our society, if you want to be accepted, is do what men do. You see killers or armies or terrorists or whatever, and the ones who want to kill are almost always men. Women do it too, but it's way more men than women. Women would never lead genocides, or shuffle people into concentration camps. We're not bloodthirsty."

I think about the Cabin Massacre, about Diane's body lying among the dozen bodies of men. "You might have a point," I admit.

"I know I do," Kendra says relentlessly. "Take violent crime. People act like violent crime is a race thing and then, when they feel bad about being racist, they cover themselves by saying it's economic. Or they blame it on guns. The truth is, it's not race or money or weapons. It's a sexual difference. Violent criminals are almost always men. Women are raped, not rapists. Women aren't the violent criminals. Men make movies and write books and *make* women do that, so men will like them, because then women are more like men. It's bullshit. For a woman to do what men do, she'd have to be a self-hating sociopath." Kendra finishes talking. The class is quiet.

Lucy has set the book down and is staring at me.

"Are you, like, a lesbian?" Simon asks Kendra.

Some men in the class laugh. The women look uncomfortable. Kendra scowls.

"Enough of that, Simon," I say, and I turn my attention away from Lucy. "Back to Kendra's point. I'm curious. Who in here likes Maria?"

Hands lift. More come from men, but some women raise their hands as well. Kendra sits with her arms crossed over her chest.

"Can I ask a question?" Ashley asks. "What kind of female character would you have liked, Kendra?"

Kendra rubs her chin. "I don't know. Maybe a woman who was interesting, someone I could relate to."

"But they're in a war," soft-spoken Chris counters. "And Maria seems like she's seen a lot of bad shit. How can you expect to relate to her?"

"Maybe relate is the wrong word," Kendra says. "I just want them to be real people. I want to feel their pain."

"That's weird," Simon comments.

Kendra doesn't turn around to face him. She just shrugs. Lucy's gone back to her book.

The discussion continues until class ends, and as students are leaving, Lucy walks up to me.

"Moira's outside," she says.

"Why?"

Lucy shrugs. "Just said she was outside."

I take my satchel and we head down the stairs and out into the parking lot.

"Hey," Moira says, leaning against my truck.

Right away, I can tell something's off. Moira always looks confident and calm, but now she seems uneasy, like something's loosened inside her.

Lucy senses it too. "You okay?"

Moira looks around. The parking lot is fairly crowded, but all of the cars around us are empty. Still, she keeps her voice low. "Switch and Daniel were attacked."

I look at Lucy. Her expression doesn't change. "Are they okay?"

Moira nods. "They're fine. Daniel was taking her to meet the Judge and they got jumped."

"How'd anyone know they were going to see the Judge?" Lucy asks.

Moira shakes her head. "I'm not sure. All I know is that we need be a lot more careful. Anyway, I wanted to give you something. It's in my trunk."

That sounds suspicious, and I can tell Lucy thinks so too. "What is it?"

Moira reaches into her handbag and I hear a click a few cars away. I hadn't noticed her BMW was so close. We walk over. Moira looks around then lifts the trunk's lid.

"What the fuck is that?" I ask.

"It's a machine gun," Moira replies.

Lucy reaches in and touches the black frame. "It's an MG4," she clarifies.

"Are you kidding? We don't need a—"

"Lower your voice!" Moira hisses.

"I'm not taking a freaking machine gun! I already have a gun."

"This is safer."

"She has a point," Lucy says.

"We have different definitions of safe. I'm not taking that." I close the trunk. "It's bad enough that I have a Glock and two assassins in my house. I'm not turning it into an armory. Thanks, but no thanks."

Moira and Lucy look at each other.

"We'll be fine," Lucy tells her.

Some students are headed our way.

"All right," Moira says reluctantly. "Just watch yourself." She opens her door and climbs inside her sedan.

Lucy is staring at the students as they approach.

"Are you all right?" I ask her.

She blinks and looks away. "Why wouldn't I be?"

"Because someone tried to kill your sister. That doesn't bother you?"

"Only if they had. Come on, let's get in your truck."

We climb into the cab and Lucy says, "Follow her."

"One of the students?"

"Moira."

"Why?"

"Because my sister just got jumped and Moira shouldn't be alone. We need to keep an eye on her, make sure she's safe."

It's not a bad point. We follow Moira out of the parking lot and down Eastern Avenue. I stay a few cars behind her.

We end up in Hampden, Baltimore's largest collec-

tion of slurred accents, beehived hairdos, Elvis collecti-
bles, window-framed Virgin Marys, marble porches, pink
flamingos, and horn-rimmed glasses.

"Someone's following her," Lucy says.

"You mean besides me?"

Lucy gives me an annoyed look. "The Escape. Two
cars ahead."

It's a small Ford Escape with deeply-shaded windows and out-of-state Pennsylvania plates. Moira turns
on Gilman, a tiny road with row houses on one side and
trees on the other. She pulls into a space and the SUV
pulls into a different one a few cars away. I stop at the
corner and watch Moira open her door and climb outside.
She walks to her porch and starts hunting in her handbag.

A man gets out of the SUV and quickly walks toward her.

"Told you," Lucy says.

We step out of my truck.

CHAPTER 23

Moira pushes open the front door just as he reaches for her. Lucy is right behind me, and I bound up the stairs and tackle him as he turns. The momentum pushes us into Moira, carries the three of us inside, and we crash to the floor.

We scramble to our feet. Moira is shaky, her hair disheveled and eyes wide as she looks back and forth at us.

"Tom? Lucy?"

The man is squat with short brown hair, small blue eyes, and a nose so bulbous it looks like it's just been punched. He reaches behind himself and closes the door. Then he pulls out a small stick from his pocket, shakes his wrist, and a metal baton shoots out. Moira shrinks away, disappears out of my line of sight.

My heart beats so hard it hurts.

Lucy draws her gun but the baton knocks it out of her hand and sends it flying across the room. She steps forward and the man swings the baton at her head. She ducks and grabs him around his waist, but he elbows her in the back and knees her in the stomach. Her arms drop. She grunts and falls backward to the floor.

I rush him. The man spins around and drops to one knee. His baton smacks into the side of my leg. He rises and, as he does, he slaps the baton against my stomach and slams it into my shoulder. The air is knocked out of me. I stagger forward, holding my shoulder, and sink to the ground.

Lucy rises. She lifts her hands in a boxing stance, but winces as she does. She and the man circle each other.

He jumps toward her, swinging the baton, but Lucy jumps back. She tries to punch him with her left hand and the baton snakes out to meet her fist, but then her left disappears and she hits him full in the face with her right. The man looks more surprised than hurt, but swings the baton toward her again. Lucy watches him, steps to the side as the baton misses her, then rakes her fingers down his face.

Blood wells from red lines over his forehead. He cries out, steps back, and stumbles. Lucy approaches him and he reaches down. I spot a gun strapped to his ankle, lift myself up, and dive toward him. He takes my weight and rolls me onto my back. I feel the cold metal baton pressing down on my neck. I look up at him, my feet kicking, eyes bulging.

Two fists crash into either of his ears and he falls off.

Lucy takes his baton and helps me up. The man struggles to stand and she slashes the baton across his bloody face. He falls back, unconscious.

We stare down at him, breathing hard. Then we look at Moira. She's standing by an entrance to the kitchen, a knife in her hand.

"Do you need my help?" she asks.

ఴఴఴ

I've just finished tying him up when Switch walks in. She and her sister are both wearing black jeans and unzipped black denim jackets with black T-shirts underneath.

"What happened to you two?" she asks.

"Didn't you get jumped?" I ask back.

"Uh huh."

"You don't seem..." I turn to Lucy. "She doesn't seem fazed."

"Are you all right?" Lucy asks her sister.

"I dunno. How's you?"

"We're fine."

And we are. The pain from the hits isn't bad. My shoulder is sore but, otherwise, I feel okay. I figure it's probably the adrenaline, and I'll be sore and bruised tomorrow.

The man's head lolls back and his eyes open a crack then squeeze shut.

"Fuck you," he says thickly.

Lucy turns toward Moira. "Do you have a pair of pliers?"

"In the hall closet."

"Can I have them?"

"Why?"

"Because," Lucy looks at him, "you're not going to talk, are you?"

His eyes stay closed.

Moira looks at Lucy, then leaves.

"What's your name?" Lucy asks.

Switch is peering at something underneath the sofa.

The man stays quiet.

"What's your name?" Lucy asks again.

Nothing.

Lucy chews a nail and studies him.

Moira walks back in the room with a thin black bag.

Lucy unrolls it to reveal a sleeve of tools. She pulls out the pliers.

"You probably want to leave," Lucy informs us.

Moira doesn't wait around. She heads out. I wonder if she's seen something like this before.

"I'm staying," I tell Lucy, although leaving does seem like a good idea.

Lucy doesn't argue. "Switch, go with Moira."

Switch bounds to her feet and leaves.

I'm not sure why I stay. Maybe it's because I know how dangerous it is not to see something like this through to the end. What if I leave and this man overpowers Lucy and escapes? He doesn't know who I am, but he knows what I look like. He might find me. He might tell others in the Eastmen about me.

Or maybe it's because I know what's going to happen to him, and part of me doesn't want it to happen.

"Give me your hand," Lucy tells him. Switch giggles from just outside the room.

The man doesn't move.

Lucy takes the pliers and positions herself behind him. She crouches down, lifts his shirt, and squeezes the pliers over a pinch of skin on the back of his arm.

The pliers twist.

He cries out and his body shakes so violently that the chair teeters over. He crashes to the floor.

"Tell her your name," I urge him.

The man just whimpers.

Lucy grabs a rag from the kitchen counter and stuffs it into his mouth.

"This part is going to hurt," she says.

"I don't think we need to do it like this," I tell her. "There's a better way."

She ignores me. "What's your name?"

The moans don't stop. He shakes his head.

"Grab his hand," Lucy tells me. "Stretch out his fingers."

"I can't." My voice sounds distant.

Lucy sighs, grabs his hand, and forces him to straighten his thumb. She places his thumb in between the pliers' metal jaws and squeezes. "Feel that?" she asks. "Feel how they're right over your knuckle?"

Dizziness is approaching me, a dark storm rushing over the horizon.

"Tell me your name," Lucy says.

Still nothing.

I'm a father, I think. *I have a daughter.*

Lucy stomps her heel down on the pliers.

I hear a splintering crunch, like the sound from stepping on a pinecone. I turn away so quickly that my neck hurts.

When I look back, Lucy is crouched and staring into his red puffed face.

"Your name?" she asks him, and pulls out the rag. "Come on."

I look at his thumb, warily, worried it's been cut off. The thumb is still attached, but the tip is bent at a strange angle.

His eyes are closed.

"He passed out?" I ask.

"Uh huh," Lucy answers.

Moira is standing in the doorway. She looks at the three of us, her face white.

"Are they here?" Lucy asks.

"The cars are outside."

"Whose cars?"

"Judge's men," Lucy says. "I called them."

"What's going to happen to him?" I ask.

"He's going to talk," Lucy says, "and then he's going to die. Tom, head home. We'll be there in a bit."

I stand slowly, roughly. It feels like I've been kneeling for hours.

Moira and I walk out of the room and pass Switch sitting by the door. She's covering her mouth to hide her laughter.

"Whose place is this?" I ask Moira.

"It belonged to my father."

Neither of us say anything else. I head out the door, close it firmly behind me.

Outside, the dying sunlight has turned the day a pale, sickened white. I walk down the porch steps, ignoring the sedans with tinted windows on either side of the house.

I don't understand what I'm feeling.

I had thought I'd feel guilt or shock after the Cabin Massacre and, instead, I felt nothing. Guilt had never come. I'd thought, back then, that the absence of guilt was a phase, some way of coping with a situation I couldn't understand. Now I wonder if this state is actually a person I could become. A person able to push his emotions down, able to forget those emotions.

A person who understands and accepts evil.

CHAPTER 24

Switch

I wave bye, bye, *bye* to Broken Thumb Man.

"Come on," Lucy says. "Let's go to Tom's."

I walk past Moira Mack and follow Lucy outside. We get into the van. Lucy starts it and off we go.

"Are you sure you're okay?" Lucy asks me.

I scratch my head. *Scritch, scritch.*

"Hey!" Lucy says. "You sure you're all right?"

"I dunno."

And then she doesn't say anything. And I don't either. And we drive. And I close my eyes.

Lucy shakes me awake.

"There's a sedan I haven't seen parked on Tom's block," she tells me. "Some guy is sitting inside."

"What huh why?"

"Come on, Switch, pay attention." Lucy's voice is full of thorns. "Ten cars down."

Lucy pushes open her door and sneaks out. I do the same, playing that little game where I try to be quieter than her.

We stop behind a big car.

"Do you see it?" Lucy asks.

I peek around the corner and there it is. I can see his moonhead over the seat.

"You seen that car here before?" Lucy asks me.

"I dunno."

"Yeah. Me neither."

We wait for another car to slide past.

"Go now," Lucy says. "Stay safe."

I run out from the car and down a different block and then slow to a skip. I look back at Lucy and she looks *mad* so I stop skipping and walk. A fat man and a fat woman step out of their house and look at me.

"Hello, good day," I tell them, and I look back at Lucy so she can see my good manners. But Lucy's gone.

I turn around the corner, hurry up the street, then go right so I can get back to the car where Moonhead is sitting. I see his car and stick my hands into my pockets. He looks out the window, sees me, and then tries to act like he doesn't. But I see him shifting around and being all suspicious silly.

I walk over to his car and stick my face against his window. He's bent, reaching for the gun on his ankle.

Lucy tap tap taps the other window with her gun, tells him to open the doors. They snap open. She climbs into the passenger seat. Me, I get in back.

"Who are you?" he asks. He's scared.

"A couple of pissed-off girls looking for a good time," Lucy tells him. "I think we found it."

CHAPTER 25

Tom

The attacks must have distracted the twins because they don't come home. I'm finally free of my watchdogs, even if it's just for a little bit. Maybe they trust me, now that I've literally fought alongside them.

The ache in my shoulder has largely subsided, but my nerves are jumpy. Something about the empty house makes them worse, like the volume raised on a sad piece of music.

I walk into the kitchen, pull open the fridge, grab a few leaves of lettuce and some small carrots for the rabbit.

I head upstairs, turning on every light that I pass, and into Julie's bedroom. I drop the food into the rabbit's cage. Bananas hops forward and eats hungrily.

I leave the rabbit but keep the light on and peek into Switch and Lucy's room. It's as plain as a monk's closet. Suitcase under the bed, black clothes hanging in the closet. Nothing else.

Downstairs again.

I sit in front of the television, pick up my phone and send Ruth a text. *Dave home?*

A few moments later. *Dave's@hotel. Julie just went to bed. Why?*

ⱰⱰⱰ

The next time I text Ruth, I'm parked down the street from her house. I left a note for Lucy and Switch, telling them where I'd gone and that I would be back soon. And then I'd buried the phone for Garrett under that loose cobblestone in my backyard.

I'm outside your front door, I text.

Jesus, Tom, she replies.

I leave my car, look around, and don't see anyone out. Going to Ruth's house isn't that suspicious an act, considering Julie is staying here, but I don't want to draw attention to myself.

Ruth opens the door before I knock. "Is everything okay?"

"Why's Dave at a hotel?"

"We got into a fight."

"About what?"

She shakes her head. I don't press.

"I miss you," I tell her.

I want to tell her more, to tell her that after watching that man get tortured, there was a loneliness in me deeper than anything I've felt. I need to escape, to slip into someone else, disappear inside their skin.

Ruth glances behind herself. "You came all the way here to tell me you missed me?"

"Well, I want to do more than tell you."

She closes the door behind her. "You remember Julie's upstairs, right? In the bedroom next to mine?"

"Yep. And I also remember you have that guest bedroom downstairs."

Ruth shakes her head, but smiles and moves her body closer to mine. "We can't."

"Sure, we can. I believe in you."

She kisses me lightly. I hold the kiss, put my hands on her hips, and pull her body in. The kiss deepens. We lean farther into the dark, and that man's cries from this afternoon grow farther away.

Ruth breaks away. "We can't do anything," she says, but her fingers are playing with my belt.

I kiss her again and let my hands slide under her shirt and trace her back.

"Okay," she relents. "But be quiet."

Ruth leads me inside. We peek around the corner of the entrance way, up the empty stairs, then hurry across to another hall, past the kitchen, den, and living room until we reach the guest bedroom. Ruth pulls me into the room after her. I close and lock the door.

"Julie's asleep, right?"

"Yeah," Ruth whispers back. "Come here."

I follow her to the bed. She lifts off her shirt as she walks and drops it on the floor. Moonlight burns through the blinds, slices her bare skin.

ℰℛℰℛ

Ruth's head is on my shoulder, her hand on my chest, her leg draped over mine. We breathe hard, but quietly.

"What time is it?"

"Probably been an hour since I got here."

"Did you like it like that?" she asks. "Hushed?"

"It was kind of fun," I tell her. "I liked sneaking around."

"Aren't we always sneaking around?"

"Tonight was different."

"Hmm," Ruth says lazily. Her hand runs up my chest. "You think this will ever be more?"

"At first," I admit, "no. I thought it was just something we both needed. I didn't expect it to last more than once or twice."

I feel her nod.

"Now," I continue, "I don't see how it couldn't be more. What we have isn't enough for me."

"Me either," Ruth says quietly. "I think about you a lot more than I let on. And I'm happy when I do. A kind of happiness I haven't felt for a long time. Ever since..." She stops. "It's just been a long time."

I close my eyes.

"But what do we do?" she asks. "Do I just leave Dave and move in with you?"

"Why not? It'd be easy on Julie, at least."

"I don't know about that. I hate the idea of hurting Dave. I know I should probably end things. Sometimes I think about this and can't believe it's me. I'm not the type to have an affair."

"It doesn't feel wrong to me," I counter. I hold Ruth close and kiss her. She lies on me, her warm skin soft. I still want to sink into her, submerge myself, get closer than physically possible.

"Dad?" Julie asks.

We freeze.

Ruth shoves herself off me and scrambles to the other side of the bed. I sit up. The lamp flashes on and I hear a crash.

The crash comes from Ruth, who scrambled too far

and fell off the bed. She picks herself up and searches for her clothes.

Knocks on the bedroom door. "Dad? Aunt Ruth?" Alarm turns her voice shrill.

It's amazing how fast we get dressed. I look at Ruth and I try to think of an excuse to tell Julie, but there's no time. The longer we wait, the worse it is. Ruth and I lock eyes.

She opens the door.

"Julie?" she asks. "What are you doing up?"

Julie doesn't answer. She just looks back and forth at us, wearing glasses and dressed in a T-shirt and shorts with her hair disheveled from sleep.

"Dad?"

"You should be asleep," Ruth says emptily.

"Listen," I say, trying to take charge. "Go back to your room. We'll be right there."

Julie doesn't move. "After you finish fucking?"

It's the first time I've ever heard her swear, but the word clearly isn't unfamiliar to her.

"Julie," Ruth says, still trying to assert some authority, "you can't speak to us that way."

"You think *I'm* the one who—" Julie begins, indignantly.

"It's all right," I interrupt her. "It's all right. Julie, I'm sorry you found out like this. Your aunt and I wanted a better way to tell you." I pause to gauge how things are going. Not well. "Believe me," I continue. "Your aunt and I never wanted to hurt—"

"No," Julie says angrily. "You can't say that. You can't say you never meant to hurt me. Because then you wouldn't have done this."

Ruth starts to speak, but looks to me for help instead. I'm not sure what to say.

Maybe it's the late evening or the rush of everything

that's happened, but I'm not even sure what Julie is mad about.

She's probably upset that she didn't know. The same way I was upset about the distance between us ever since she started dating Anthony.

"Listen, honey," I start, "I know why you're up—"

"It's like you don't give a fuck about Mom," Julie says.

"What?"

"Mom," Julie says again. "What do you think she'd say if she saw you two?"

Ruth and I just look at her.

"Her husband and her sister," Julie says. "How would any woman feel?"

Something in me shifts, unmoors.

"You always told me how you loved her, both of you," Julie goes on, bitterly. "But every time you're together like this, you decrease her."

"Desecrate," Ruth murmurs.

Julie stalks out of the room.

"I'll go after her," I say after a few moments.

Ruth doesn't respond. She stays still, sitting up, quietly crying.

I want to say something, but I'm not sure what. I head out of the bedroom.

I walk over to the stairs but, instead of walking up them, I sit down heavily on the dark bottom step.

Renee.

I feel her now, just as I had in the woods.

At night, she'd wake late and watch TV at our kitchen table with its lousy yellow tablecloth, and I sometimes woke and joined her. We'd eat awful food and those times and these memories were ours.

Ours.

I'd buy roses for Renee, small gifts, pink roses always, her favorites. She wrote letters to me. I liked those letters. They were like pages from a diary, plain, unadorned, not trying to be poetic or even having any idea of how to do so. They were only honest, and I knew the poetry in that. She always smiled after I kissed her. Everything that happened with us happened in a rush, but it was a long bursting rush, like a lap sprinted; we rushed together. "You remind me of old romantic songs," I'd tell her, and she'd smile under those shadowed eyes.

Back then, life was like songs with strings.

I'm drowning in memories, struggling to breathe. Rising to my feet feels like swimming to the surface for air. I walk to the door, open it, and step outside to the same porch I'd stood on an hour earlier.

Julie's not there.

Someone else is.

"It's time to go," Daniel tells me.

I'm not sure what to say, not even sure what's happening.

He lifts his shirt to show me the gun tucked in his waistband.

"Don't make me do this here," Daniel says, and he nods toward the open door. "Not where they'll find you."

"I don't understand. What do you want?"

"I'm taking you to the Judge," he tells me. "He wants to talk to you about your pals in the FBI."

CHAPTER 26

Daniel

I don't know anyone in the FBI," Tom keeps saying, his wrists handcuffed and the cuffs looped around a bar under the dashboard, in the van that everyone calls Diane's van, and we always will, no matter how long she's been dead, because you don't forget people like Diane easy, not like I always forgot the name of that skinny guy who'd been her partner, Bird Dog or something? Diane stuck out.

"I don't know anyone—" Tom starts to say again.

"Tell it to the Judge," I snarl, and I feel good as we drive.

Better than I did when we were supposed to set up Switch and I had my gun out and I couldn't even lift it as she looked at me and I let her take it from my shaky hand. That was a total giant failure and it's a good thing nobody from the Eastmen saw me freeze.

And today I'd just inhaled a giant bong an hour before they'd called me and told me to pick Tom up and told me a couple of places he'd probably be. I'd worried

he'd recognize my voice from the shop but he hadn't
known who I was when I drove him to that meeting in
Edgewater. Good thing, because I'd have put a bullet in
his head.

But even in my mind that tough guy shit doesn't
sound right for me.

"Why does the Judge think I'm working against
him?" Tom whines.

I don't answer because now I'm wondering whether
the Judge is going to make me kill Tom. I just tell Tom to
shut the fuck up and he finally does.

We leave Baltimore behind, those high lit windows
of hotels and offices that make me feel sad as fuck to imagine someone in there alone. I hate images like that,
those lonely spirals.

We turn onto the interstate.

"Where are you taking me?" Tom asks, even though
I'd told him to shut the fuck up. But that's okay because
now I want the conversation.

"Same place I took you before."

"Why?" he asks, trying and failing to keep the fear
out of his voice. "I told you I don't know anyone in the
FBI."

"You just stood there when I handcuffed you," I tell
him instead of answering but I don't remember what he'd
asked anyway because it's hard as shit to concentrate after a pound of weed passes through your lungs. "I thought
you'd at least try to escape."

"You had the gun," he points out.

"You know where I'm taking you. You know what's
going to happen." I shift in my seat, trying not to let this
one memory come charging back but I can't stop it and
my hand tightens over the wheel.

"Couple of months ago I broke into this guy's house
to bring him to Mack and the guy's wife is there. And

this fucking guy is so scared he begs me to bring his wife with him. She's crying and screaming and he's got her wrist and won't let go. She's digging her nails into him and they're both screaming. And he must have known that if he brought her then she'd be done in too. But I don't think he wanted anything bad to happen to her. I just don't think he wanted to face what was coming alone."

That lonely spiral.

CHAPTER 27

Julie

Ruth is calling for me but like I give a fuck.
"I'm going out!" I scream at her, wherever she is.
I storm outside with my coat, grab the door with both hands, and slam it as hard as I can.

I walk down the porch steps, expecting her to run after me. She doesn't. I don't know where my dad is. I head down to the sidewalk and he's not there. Just quiet rich houses and parked cars and a van driving away.

He was fucking Ruth when he was married to mom.

This is the second time I've caught him with Ruth, which is disgusting and is totally going to put me on a therapist's couch someday. I remember when I asked him about the first time, like, three or four years ago. He denied it, of course, and said he'd never cheated on Mom—but come on. Easy to see this has been happening for a while. I just can't believe either of them would do this.

I walk to the end of the block and there's a kids' park across the street. I head over, sit on a bench and stare at the swings.

I plan to sit there moodily, maybe all night, and then have someone find me in the morning and ask what happened. Maybe Ruth. And she'll tell me that she's sorry for doing this, and that she shouldn't have said Anthony couldn't come over the other day, and that she needs to treat me like an adult.

I pull out my phone and text Anthony. *Srsly call me*

And then I text some more people, sitting there in the cold, and my nose starts running and I'm starting to think that Ruth is probably freaking out looking for me.

I turn off my phone, look up and *shit*, there's a man standing in front of me.

CHAPTER 28

Tom

D id Julie see me taken at gunpoint? The idea tears my mind. My hands squeeze until my nails push into my palms. I try to relax, to stay calm.

"So this is your job?" I ask, making conversation to try to clear my mind. "You bring people to the Judge?"

"For now," Daniel says.

"Have you ever killed anyone?"

His shoulders stiffen. "Not yet."

I have to ask, "Did you see my daughter?"

"When?"

"When you picked me up just now. Was my daughter outside the house?"

Daniel lightly shakes his head, and I get the feeling that his mind is somewhere else.

"You have anything you want to tell your kid?" he asks. "I can have Lucy say something."

"No. I don't have anything."

CHAPTER 29

Julie

D id I scare you?" the man asks.

"No," I say, and then, "maybe a little."

He holds up his hands. "Just taking a walk. Blowing off steam."

It's like bells and whistles are going off inside my head, and something deep inside me wants to run away, but I don't.

CHAPTER 30

Tom

D aniel pushes opened his door and walks around to my side of the van. The street is quiet. No house windows look out onto us, no cars drive past. We're at the same house in Edgewater he took me to a few nights earlier.

Daniel slides my door open.

"This is when people get scared," he says.

He undoes my cuffs with one hand and keeps his gun trained on me with the other.

"In the house."

I walk ahead of him, through the garage and into the kitchen.

I hadn't paid attention to the kitchen the last time I'd been here, but now I get a good look. A long wooden table is surrounded by chairs, drapes curve over closed blinds, silverware gleams in a rack next to the sink. But there's an unused sense to everything, as if this is a model home, a place people visit but don't live.

The narrow door that leads to the basement opens

and Lucy and Switch walk out. I can see a small haze of yellow light before Switch shuts the door.

"Switch and I found someone waiting outside your house," Lucy tells me.

My stomach tightens, but I try not to look worried. "Yeah? Who?"

"An FBI agent. Name of Peterson."

Is that Garrett's partner? I shrug. "That doesn't mean I'm working with him. He could have been following you and Switch."

I think it's a shrewd point, but Lucy isn't swayed.

"Tom," she says. "He had your name in his phone."

I try to remember if Peterson has ever called me. No, it's only been Garrett. But has Garrett always used his own phone?

Switch walks over to the sink.

"If the FBI did suspect I was involved in something," I offer, "and started keeping an eye on me, it makes sense they'd have my number." I pause. "The real test is if he ever called."

"He didn't," Lucy admits, and my stomach untightens a little. "But you've already failed your test."

Daniel snorts.

"I don't know what to tell you," I say, and desperation breaks my voice. "I don't know anyone in the FBI!"

"Too bad," Lucy says, and she looks at Switch. Switch ambles over and opens the door to the basement. "They could have helped you tonight."

"You want me to go down there?"

"You and your friend might as well wait for the Judge together."

"He's not my friend," I tell them, and I glance down the dark staircase. "I'm not going down there."

"You go down there or we'll gut you where you

stand," Lucy says. The words come easy.

I feel hope falling. "Why don't you believe me? I fought for Moira with you."

The three of them just look at me, then Switch turns toward her sister. I hope it's to say something on my behalf.

"Want me to tie him up too?"

"Him?" Lucy asks, and she and Daniel laugh.

Switch looks back and forth between them, then she starts laughing too. She bends over, holds her side and shrieks out, "I dunno! I dunno!"

They quiet down, but it takes a few minutes. Lucy rubs her eyes. "All right, Tom, into the basement. You walk down the stairs or we throw you down them."

"Or gut him?" Switch asks hopefully.

"That's right."

I slowly start walking down the stairs. The door shuts behind me.

CHAPTER 31

Julie

The man definitely scares me, maybe because it's hard to get a good look at him in the dark. All I can tell is that he's wearing jeans and a leather jacket. And he's big. Like, really big.

He walks over to a tree and leans against it. He's so deep in the shadows that I can't really see him at all.

And I want to run, but I don't.

Something occurs to me. I'm that chick in the horror movies who walks toward the monster in the basement.

"Why are you blowing off steam?" I ask.

He laughs a little. "Tough day at work," he tells me. "Why are you sitting out here in the middle of the night? That's not very safe."

I rub my hands together. It's colder now. "I had a tough day too."

"Tell me about it," he says.

CHAPTER 32

Tom

The basement is cold and smells of stale water. My footsteps echo as I descend.

A single light bulb hangs above a chair in the middle of the room. A man is tied to it, his back to me.

I stop, one foot on the bottom step, the other on the basement floor.

"Hello?" I call out. My mouth is so dry it's tough to get the word out.

He doesn't move.

The basement's walls are buried in the dark, but the room seems smaller than I remember. I walk to the chair and it takes me a moment to recognize the man sitting in it. It's Garrett's partner, but his face is disfigured, nearly beyond recognition. The skin looks like it's been chewed and his complexion is discolored, with purple splotches staining his cheeks and forehead, as if his face is a faded map. One eye stares out from bruised, scarred flesh. His lips are covered in cuts and dried blood.

"What'd they do to you?" I ask.

"Everything," Peterson says, his voice faint.

I walk back around Peterson, kneel behind him, and try and loosen the ropes binding his wrists. But the knots are thin and tight, and I can't unties them.

His head lolls back and he looks sideways at me.

"I'm sorry," I tell him. "I can't get your hands free."

He doesn't say anything.

"Is there any other way out of here?"

Peterson shakes his head. "I don't think so. Just the stairs."

I lean in close and whisper, "They know everything."

"I know," Peterson says, his voice low and hoarse. "I shouldn't have let them catch me. Got careless."

"Is there any way we can escape? Anything we can do?"

"Not as long as I'm tied up."

I stand and head into the shadows. "I'll see if there's anything I can use to cut the ropes."

"If you find something," he calls out, and it sounds like an effort for him to speak louder, "we can use it as a weapon."

I walk into the dark with my hands outstretched until I touch the cold wall. I bend down, one hand on the floor and the other on the wall, hoping my fingers pass over something.

"I don't think you'll have much luck," Peterson says despondently.

I reach a corner and head left. My fingers pass over occasional rough spots, and I realize they're stains from something sticky. Blood.

CHAPTER 33

Julie

He's really smart," I tell the man. "He reads so much more than I do. Like, I told him I was really into *Twilight*, and he told me that I should read this other guy named Stalker or something, because he, like, invented vampires. But he's also into sports. Like football. He's on the JV team, but he really wants to make Varsity. I think—"

"Excuse me," the man says, and his voice is all strained.

I hear something shuffling around, and then there's a light and I see a phone.

He looks at me. "This is an important phone call."

"Okay."

I'm not sure if he wants me to leave or something, but he starts talking. "He did?...Okay...That's good...No, not anymore...Yes, you can..."

I get bored and start thinking about Anthony again. And I'm so deep in thought that I don't even realize the stranger has stopped talking.

CHAPTER 34

Tom

I reach the next corner and head to my left. I keep an eye on Peterson, sitting underneath that single light bulb. An idea occurs to me.

"Maybe we can break the chair, smash that light bulb, and try and take them in the dark."

"How many are there?" Peterson asks.

"Three. And the Judge is coming."

"I can barely move after what they did to me," he says, "and I take it you're not a fighter?"

Another corner. I continue my crouched walk along the final wall.

"I go to the gym," I tell him. "Do pull-ups. That's about it." I reach the stairs and sit on the bottom step.

"We have to talk our way out of this," Peterson tells me. "That's our only move."

"And tell them what?"

"Tell them we don't know each other. That'll save you, and maybe save me. Or maybe if they believe you, you can escape and come back for me."

"I dunno," I tell him. "Even if I make it out of here, they'll kill you before they come after me."

"We don't have a choice," Peterson says, and his voice has hardened. "This is the only way to get out of this, to keep our families safe."

"It's not going to work," I insist. "I know these people. It's all or nothing. If they think I'm working with the FBI, then nothing's going to help me."

"Do you understand what's going to happen?" Peterson asks, still whispering, but with increasing urgency. "I know these people too. They're not going to stop with us. They'll go after our families, after people we love. Do you understand that? We have to try my plan."

Fear rustles in me. He's right. Julie knows Lucy and Switch. If I disappear, it'll be reported to the police. And if the police ask Julie what happened, she's going to tell the cops about the drug-addicted woman who was staying with us. And her twin sister.

And if I know that will happen, then the Judge's people definitely know it.

Peterson is still talking excitedly, almost incoherently. "...so you tell them you don't know me and when you get by the door, you run out and go to a neighbor or anyone and you tell them—" He stops talking and turns his head toward me as I stand. "Are you going upstairs?"

I don't answer. I don't say anything because I can't think about what I'm doing. I can't think about it because, if I do, I won't do it. All I can think about is Switch and Lucy going to my house after I'm dead and finding Julie there.

And that's all I think about as I kneel behind Peterson and wrap my arm around his neck.

He lets out a small shout before I cover his mouth with my other hand. I squeeze my arm around his neck as his body kicks.

Somehow my thumb ends up in his mouth and I feel his teeth sink into my flesh. I cry out and pull him backward and the chair collapses on me. Something snaps.

I'm worried it's part of my body, but nothing hurts except my thumb. And then I wonder if it's Peterson' neck, since he's not moving. I push him off me and crawl to my feet, walk a few steps and something rolls underneath me.

I pick it up. A piece of wood.

The chair must have broken when we fell.

I turn and Peterson is on his feet, hands still tied behind him.

He hurls himself at me and our bodies slam together. We fall to the floor and he bites my chest. Fire races through me. I shove him away.

I climb to my feet but Peterson is on the ground, rolling, trying to stand without his hands. I step back, feel part of the broken chair underneath me, and I pick it up. Peterson looks up and I smash the wood into his face.

He cries out and the cry turns to a gurgle. He looks up, frantically, and I hit him again. This time, he stays on the ground.

I stand over him, bent over and breathing heavily, as he sluggishly moves beneath me. I close my eyes and his head pushes into my ankle.

I roll him to his back and sit over his chest.

"I'm sorry," I tell him. Tears cloud my eyes. "I'm so sorry. This isn't me."

"Please," Peterson says, his voice thick. "Please. We can tell them—"

I hear his feet scrabbling against the floor.

I lift his head and smash the back of his skull against the cement. His head bounces and he looks at me, his tongue out, his eyes frightened and desperate.

I smash his head into the floor again.
And again.
Finally, his feet stop quivering.

CHAPTER 35

Julie

The stranger steps away from the tree and into the light. He looks at me and I look back. For some reason, I'm suddenly too scared to speak. Then he just walks away.

CHAPTER 36

Tom

I crawl off Peterson and turn to my side. Nausea rushes. My stomach empties on the floor.
I stand shakily, walk slowly up the stairs.
I knock on the door. Lucy opens it.
"I told you," I say to her, "I'm on your side."

PART II

CHAPTER 37

"Why'd you kill him?" Lucy asks.

I sit at the kitchen table. Lucy and Daniel face me from the other side. Switch is in the basement with Peterson's body. I don't know where the Judge is.

"Well?" Lucy asks.

I've done too much to die now. I'm close to leaving this house, to returning to my daughter.

"I didn't think there was another way to convince you," I say to her. My voice feels strange, like it hasn't been used for weeks.

Julie. This is all for Julie. If I'm safe, she's safe. If they believe I'm innocent, she's innocent.

"I couldn't prove myself any other way," I tell Lucy. "I don't know what else I could have done."

Please let it be enough. Please.

Lucy and Daniel both look behind me. I turn as Switch emerges from the door to the basement, bent over and grunting as she drags Peterson by the legs. She backs into the room, tugs him past us, and into the garage.

We're quiet as she passes.

I can still feel his head in my hands.

Three people now. I've killed three people. Not been responsible for their deaths in some abstract way, but actually killed. Diane, Bailey, and now Peterson.

But Diane and Bailey had been murderers.

Peterson was with the FBI.

My chest cramps. Peterson was with the FBI. I've killed an innocent man. I try to think about Julie, but my mind is black.

Lucy sighs.

"Follow me," she says. She stands and heads into the garage.

I don't look back at Daniel as I follow her, but he doesn't say anything. Just stays at the table.

"Where are we going?" I ask Lucy.

Lucy ignores me, climbs into the van, and starts it.

I open the passenger door. "Is he in here?" I ask. "His body?"

Switch pokes her face out from the back. "Just me," she says.

"We're going back home," Lucy tells me. "The Judge believes you."

We pull away from the house and drive off, passing through the dark empty streets of Edgewater.

"Do you believe me?" I ask, after we've driven for a few minutes.

Lucy glances into the rearview mirror and pulls over. "Get out."

"Here?"

Lucy pushes open her door, climbs out, walks around the van, and yanks my door open. She grabs my arm and I stumble outside. She leads me away from the road, into the weeds.

I'm not sure where we are. I can see Lucy's face, but faintly, from a light post across the street.

She bends my wrist and I collapse to my knees.

"Why are you working with the FBI?" she asks.

"I'm not working with anyone," I tell her, trying to talk through pain. "I'm not!"

"Come on, Tom," she chides me, "don't lie."

"You've been with me this whole time," I insist. "You've been watching me! You'd have seen them."

"I'm not with you *all* the time," Lucy says darkly, but she lets go of my wrist.

I fall backward and clutch my arm close to my gut. "I'm not lying," I insist.

"I've done a lot of things I regret," Lucy says, and she leans close to me. I can see her dark intense eyes. "If you're lying to me," she says, "killing you won't be one of those things."

CHAPTER 38

Julie

Ruth is at the front door calling my phone when I get back to her house.

"Where were you?" she asks. "Where's your dad?"

"I went for a walk," I tell her. "I don't know where dad is. He probably went home."

That doesn't seem like the kind of thing my dad would do, but whatever. Weird night. I push past Ruth and head inside.

"Julie," Ruth says, "we need to talk."

"I have nothing to talk about."

"I do," she says. "Please." She runs up to me and catches my arm. "Please, Julie."

"Jesus, don't beg. What?"

"I know you're mad, but you can't tell my husband."

I wasn't planning on telling Dave, mainly because he always looks so pissed, but I realize she doesn't know that.

"You want me to lie?"

Ruth nods. "I'm sorry, Julie. Please. I will tell him, someday, but I don't want him to find out like this."

Sure, she's going to tell him someday.

"Uncle Dave has a right to know," I say, throwing the *uncle* in there because I know that makes me and Dave sound all close.

Ruth's hand tightens on my arm. I shake it off and turn away.

"Julie!" Ruth wails. "Please!"

And I have this idea that I want Ruth to suffer, but when I hear her voice like that, it just breaks something in me. I stop and turn to her and Ruth is on the ground, sobbing. I walk over to her and she climbs to her knees and holds me around the waist. She's just crying, all helplessly, holding onto me like the ground fell away beneath her.

I think about what she's doing with my dad, and I just want to turn that knife. But I can't help the tears coming to my eyes.

I kneel and hold her.

CHAPTER 39

Tom

It's the following afternoon and all I've been able to think about is the wet thick sound of Peterson's head slamming into the basement floor. I blink and look at Switch, sitting in the back row of my Hemingway class, smiling at the closed door. The students can't tell the difference between the twins, but Switch's wild eyes and unpredictable behavior set her so far apart from Lucy's stoicism that I never get the sisters confused.

Then again, the students don't even know they're twins. They just assume it's one woman with a strange personality.

"I feel like everybody's going to die in this book," Chris says.

"Why do you say that?" I ask distantly.

After the twins and I arrived home last night, I'd texted Ruth to apologize for disappearing and to make sure Julie was okay. All I received back was a brief reply. *Julie ran out then came back later. She's ok. We wondered what happened 2u.*

I texted back. *Can I talk to her?*

She said later.

"No one's safe," Chris continues.

"What do you mean?" Kendra asks.

"Well, it's third person, right?" Chris asks. "That means the narrator isn't a character. Like, if it was first person, then you'd know he's safe."

This conversation constantly comes up in my literature classes. "A first-person narrator can die," I tell them. "All it means is that he or she wasn't really the person telling the story."

My stomach feels shaky. I don't want to talk about death. Maybe Hemingway wasn't the best choice.

"Um, professor?" Kendra asks and points.

I look to where Kendra is pointing along with the rest of the class, and I see that Switch has taken out a long knife and is sharpening it on a thin whetstone.

"Lucy!" I call out, surprised I'd remembered to call Switch her sister's name in front of the students. "Put that away."

Switch grins at me, lifts her pants leg, and slips the knife into a sheath.

"We're not allowed to have weapons on campus," Simon announces, and he looks at me.

"Keep that in your pants for the rest of the day," I order Switch, and she gives me a giant wink. "And wait outside," I add. Switch stands and ambles out.

"Jesus Christ," Chris says, after she's gone. "She's going to be a teacher?"

"Jails have teachers," I respond, but no one laughs.

I can still feel Peterson's skin.

"I was wondering what people thought about Robert's relationship with Maria," Ashley says, changing the subject.

"It's okay," Kendra says. "For what she is."

"Yeah," Simon says. "I didn't think much about it. And the sex wasn't that hot."

"It's the only good thing for him in the book," I tell them quietly.

"What do you mean?" Ashley asks.

"What else does Robert have going for him?" I answer. "His cause? You can see it's not what he wants it to be. Maria is the one pure thing he has and he needs her desperately."

The class is staring at me.

"Anyway, class dismissed. Check your syllabus for the next assignment."

The students start to file out and the phone buried in my bag buzzes. Garrett. I hurry out, tell Switch I need to stop in the restroom, hand her my other phone, and walk in.

"Starks," he says, "do you know what happened to Peterson?"

"What do you mean?" I whisper.

"He's in the hospital," Garrett says. "In a coma."

The phone is heavy in my hand.

Peterson is alive.

"They did a number on him," Garrett continues. "I just got back from City Hospital, and his head looks like a car ran over it. It's touch and go."

"I see."

"Listen, we've been pussyfooting around this group, and I'm not doing it anymore. They know we're after them. I know you feel like you're in danger, and the only way to end this is to move forward. Quickly. Viciously. The gloves need to come the fuck off."

He pauses.

"Starks, you there?"

"Yeah," I tell him. "I heard you."

"What are you doing?"

"Just leaving school," I reply.

I hang up, hide the phone back in my satchel, and try to think of a way to get to the hospital.

CHAPTER 40

T he thing is," I tell Switch, "I have to meet with students privately, and no one else can be in the room."

"I'll wait outside."

I expected that answer. "Okay. It should only be for a few hours. Too bad my DVRs on the fritz. Otherwise you could watch *The Voice*. You like that show, right?"

"Your DVRs on the fritz?" Switch squeals.

I nod solemnly.

"Is there a TV here?"

"Not that I know of."

Switch looks conflicted, and I decide to make things easy for her.

"Look, I'm going to be in student-teacher meetings for a couple of hours. Why don't you head home and I'll meet you there?"

"I dunno."

"It's just two hours. I think things will be okay."

"You think so?" Switch asks uncertainly.

❧❧❧

I head to City Hospital after Switch rushes home. I've been to City once before, when a doctor detected a small heart murmur and Renee freaked out and insisted I see a cardiologist. The murmur turned out to be nothing more than an irregular heartbeat, but Renee was always overly cautious, almost paranoid. She was a worrier, and normal issues—car troubles, routine expenses, her weight—occasionally overwhelmed her.

Then again, I'm beginning to think paranoia isn't such a bad thing.

I pull into the top floor of a parking garage near the hospital and kill the engine. No other cars are near me.

I call Moira.

"Tom." Her voice is flat. "I heard about last night."

"They didn't give me a choice."

"That's what I heard."

"Did you hear what happened to Peterson?"

"No."

"He's in the hospital, in a coma."

Moira doesn't sound surprised. "How'd you hear that?"

I'd thought of an answer, because I still don't feel comfortable telling Moira about my FBI connections. "I was paranoid today, so I called the FBI and pretended I was his relative. They told me where he was."

Another pause from her. I know it's a weak story. "What I want to know," I ask, to give her something else to think about, "is how he ended up here?"

"Here?" Moira asks back. "Where are you?"

"At the hospital."

"Tom," Moira starts to say, and she sounds surprised, "don't do anything—"

I turn off the phone.

Fat round raindrops splash and break on my windshield, sliding down the glass like desperate souls slipping into hell. I'd been too occupied with thoughts of Peterson, and what he'd say if he woke, to notice the rain. Any protection I can count on from the FBI will be over if Peterson recovers and tells them what I've done. Garrett will toss me in with the rest of the Judge's men, and he won't give a shit about Julie.

Which only leaves one option.

Peterson can't wake up.

I walk through a long bridge connecting the parking garage to the hospital, and pass a thin black woman sitting at the main desk. I follow the signs to Trauma.

I'm a little worried someone might stop me, but there aren't many people walking the halls this late at night. Not that there's a reason to notice me: I'm just some guy in jeans and a gray button down shirt, wandering the halls of the hospital, looking for a man I need to kill.

My phone buzzes. I pull it out of my pocket, glance at the screen, and tuck my Bluetooth into my ear.

"What are you doing at the hospital?" Moira asks.

No one's near me but, even so, I keep my voice low. "You know what I'm doing."

"You're going to kill him?"

"Finish it, yeah."

"How? Have you thought about that?"

It's a good question, and I don't have an answer. Peterson's in a coma, so he's probably plugged into some type of machine busily monitoring him. I'll have to kill him and leave the room before an alarm sounds.

I stop to gather my thoughts in a small alcove with a water fountain and restrooms. "I don't know how I'm going to do it," I whisper. An idea occurs to me. "What about a pillow?"

"You've seen too many movies, Tom. The doctors will be able to tell."

A woman walks past me and into the bathroom. I wait for the door to close before I speak again.

"What difference does that make? They already know someone tried to kill him."

"Here's the difference," Moira tells me. "I assume you're not wearing a fake hat and mustache, right?"

"Well, no—"

"The minute you entered that hospital, you were on a camera. They got you walking through the doors, probably have you walking down a hallway or two, right?"

I hadn't thought of that. "Probably."

"If they find out that this guy was killed in his room, they're going to shut down that hospital, get tape on everyone they can, and it's not going to take long to match you as someone who used to go to my dad's store. And the hospital isn't that busy now, right?"

I step out of the alcove and glance up and down the hallway. There's not a camera here but, even though I hadn't noticed one, I'm sure there was a camera by the entrance.

But I keep walking.

"So what do I do?" I ask. "Go home?"

"Yes. Leave it to the professionals."

I enter Trauma and head to a pair of double doors marked Authorized Personnel Only.

"I can't take that chance," I tell her.

I turn off my phone and pull the Bluetooth out of my ear. I peer through the window in the door on the right and see a sleepy attendant, her elbow propped on her desk and her cheek pressed into her palm. A wide hallway with closed doors on either side is behind her.

The window on the left reveals another hall. I press my face against the glass and spot a man sitting on a chair outside one of the rooms. He's wearing jeans and the kind of polo Garrett and Peterson favor. His arms are huge, biceps the size of baby's heads.

I move away from the door, lean against a nearby wall, chew my thumbnail, and think. But I'm not thinking about the guard.

I'm thinking about Julie.

If anyone knew the extent of everything I've done, the blood of two people on my hands, and almost a third—I'd lose her. And maybe I should lose her.

I've told myself that everything I've done since hiring hit men three years ago has been in defense of me and Julie, but I can't defend my actions any more. I've been attacked, watched a man tortured, and almost killed someone, and that was just the last two days. Every problem has been life-threatening, and every solution has been violence.

The door opens and the muscular man standing outside the room steps into the hallway. He walks past without noticing me and heads to a restroom a few doors down.

I look into the glass again. The room is unattended.

CHAPTER 41

Ruth's Acura pulls up next to my truck. She kills the engine, steps outside, looks around in the same guilty fashion she always does when she sees me, and climbs inside my cab.

"So now we're meeting in empty parking garages?" Ruth asks.

"Thanks for coming," I tell her. "I'm sort of all messed up."

"You look it." She touches my arm, lets her fingers trace up my wrist. "What happened? Does it have to do with Julie?"

"Not really."

"I talked to her," Ruth tells me anyway. "She's not going to tell Dave. But you really should stop by tomorrow and see her. It took me a long time to smooth things over."

"I will. Look, there's something I need to tell you." I keep my eyes trained out the windshield as I talk. "And I've never told it to anyone. I don't even know how to start."

Her hand is still on my arm but now it feels distant. She's gone from comforting to cautious.

"Do you have herpes?" she asks.

CHAPTER 42

Switch

Bus, bus, then run up the street and I unlock open the door and fly into the den. I turn on the TV and I don't know what channel my voice is on.

"Switch?"

I turn around and Lucy is in the hall.

"Where's Tom?"

"I dunno," I say, and I turn back to the TV and go channel, channel, channel.

"Switch," Lucy says, and she comes into the room and stands in front of me, "this is important. Where's Tom?"

"I—he had meetings? He told me to come here."

Lucy looks like an axe. "What kind of meetings?"

"I dunno!"

Lucy grabs my arm and then I'm standing up. "He's at school?"

"He told me to come here, yes."

"I told you not to leave him!"

My arm hurts. Lucy raises her hand and my hand is

pressing buttons and I try to look over her shoulder at the TV. And then her hand is down on my face twice and I step backward and fall.

Lucy makes fists and I push myself away and look through her legs at the TV and then Lucy raises her fist and I hide my head.

And then she's on the ground with me.

I taste her shirt and she holds me and says, "You need to do exactly what I tell you, Switch. It's not safe. You need to do exactly what I tell you, you need to be safe..."

CHAPTER 43

Tom

I don't have herpes," I tell Ruth. "I wanted to know if you ever worry that your guilt is going to catch up to you?"

Her expression relaxes.

"What you're feeling," Ruth tells me, "is what I felt when all this first started. Men don't realize the emotions of something the same time that women do. Women realize consequences as they act."

Ruth thinks I'm talking about us, and I decide to let her think that. I'd wanted to tell her everything I was involved in, but now I'm not sure. "Maybe you're just a better person than I am," I say.

"I don't think that's true. I knew the full extent of what I was doing the entire time. You never really thought about it. I'm guilty, you're just naïve." Ruth pauses. "Well, you're also guilty."

"I don't think I felt much guilt before," I tell her.

"Some days," she says, "I don't feel that much guilt either. But that doesn't take away from how wrong this has been. The guilt you're feeling now is nothing compared to what I've—I'm the one who has looked Dave in the eye every day, who's lied to him, who's spent hours having arguments with myself to justify what we're doing. Dave has his faults, but he's never done anything like this to me."

"Every man has his secrets," I say darkly.

"Trust me, for a while I *hoped* Dave was with another woman. I've gone through his work and home computers and through his phone records and trailed him to work and there's nothing, Tom. He's unhappy, and he's alone, but he's faithful. He told me he goes to hotels so he can feel taken care of." She touches her eyes, holds her fingers there, trying to stop the tears. "Do you know how sad that is?"

I don't say anything.

"You want to know who the only good person is in this whole mess?" Her voice is hoarse. "It's not you or me. And Dave and I have been through so much—the infertility, the deaths of my sister, my parents. Tragedy can make spouses into enemies or enemies into spouses and, regardless of that path, you're bound."

"So you could never leave him?"

"I don't know," Ruth says helplessly.

"You wouldn't end things with Dave, come with me, and help me raise Julie?"

"I think you're running away from guilt," she says. "Besides, that sounds creepy. I'd be Renee."

"You're not going to be Renee. We don't have to have that life." The idea excites me. "We can leave Baltimore. Start out somewhere else. You, me, and Julie. You leave Dave and we move and never look back. We can be completely different people!"

Ruth smiles. "I like it when you get like this. It's cute."

"Because I'm right?"

"Because you're hoping for the impossible. That's one reason I fell in love with you. You always want something that's just out of reach."

"That sounds pathetic."

She shakes her head. "It's romantic. Most people just stop trying."

"So don't stop. Come with me. Let's run off somewhere, like Paris or Brazil or St. Louis. That last one if you want to stay domestic."

"If I did leave Dave," Ruth says, "then why would we have to run somewhere else? Why can't we just stay here?"

"I just think it would work better if we went away. I want to leave."

She leans over and kisses me.

"I need to think about it," Ruth says. "About everything. Because no matter what, something has to change." Now her voice is firm. "I can't lie anymore."

"I know."

Ruth reaches for the door, turns and kisses me again.

I stay in the truck after she leaves, thinking about our conversation. It went the way conversations like this always go—determined to discover new ground, ultimately unchanged, inching closer and closer to the end.

CHAPTER 44

I visit Julie the following afternoon after my morning composition class has ended. Dave answers the door. Switch is in my truck, flipping the sun visor to pass the time. There's no way I'll be able to get free from her now. When I had come from the hospital last night, Lucy had sat me down on the couch and yelled at me for twenty minutes. Switch was sulking in her bedroom, having received her scolding from her sister when she got home.

"Starks," Dave says, his voice a mixture of boredom and disdain. "What do you want?"

"Is Julie here?"

"She's upstairs," Dave replies, but doesn't move aside to let me in.

He stays leaning against the door, one arm pressed against it, sweating in basketball shorts and a tank top. I must have interrupted him mid-workout.

"I need to see her."

He eyes me a moment longer. "Come on in."

The door closing behind me reminds me of a sprung trap.

But there's no trap. Dave goes back to his workout room and I head to the stairs. I walk to the second floor.

I knock on Julie's door.

"Hon?"

No answer. I open the door and walk inside.

Julie is sitting in bed, cross-legged, a book in front of her. She looks up, pushes her hair out of her face and peers at me through her glasses.

"What's up?"

"I wanted to see how you were doing," I tell her, and I close the door behind me. "And I wanted to talk to you about the other night."

Julie looks down at her book. "What do you want to say?"

For some reason, I'm a little off-guard. "Well, I don't know. Is there anything you want to ask me?"

"I know I need to keep everything a secret. Ruth already gave me the talk."

I wish Julie would lower her voice. "She did?"

"Last night. Then again this morning. She told me she's been really confused and sad, and she needs to figure some things out. And she's sorry."

"Oh." A beat passes. "Is there anything you want to ask me?"

"Not really. I know what this is. This is one of those guy things where you try and feel better by being honest about something, and you end up feeling better but we feel worse." She looks up at me. "Right?"

I'm taken aback at how perceptive she is. "That's not what I want."

"Doesn't matter. You're just going to lie, anyway."

"I've never lied to you."

Incredulity crosses her face. "You don't think this is all one lie?"

My daughter, I realize, is a much better person than I am. "I'm sorry," I tell her. "I'm sorry that you found out this way. I wish it hadn't happened like this."

Julie sighs and closes her book, a popular young adult novel I'd probably hate, featuring vampires or werewolves or some shit like vampwolves. "That's the same thing Ruth told me."

"She meant it. So do I."

"This really wasn't happening when Mom was alive?"

"Absolutely not," I say. "I was never with anyone but your mother."

Julie grunts.

"I'm not lying to you."

"Do you love each other? You and Ruth?"

I'm not sure what to say. "I don't know," I answer. And then, "Hon, why are you crying?"

Julie wipes away her tears and holds out her hand to stop me from approaching.

"Because," she says, her voice broken and quiet, "I feel like you left me and Mom behind. I feel like you don't care about anyone but yourself."

I protest, but part of me welcomes the accusation, believes it. "I don't understand."

The tears are still coming. "Jesus, Dad, you really don't get it."

"I'm sorry, I don't." I pause. "It comes with being a man."

Julie doesn't smile, doesn't even come close to smiling.

"Is this about me being with someone else?" I ask.

She shakes her head. "That doesn't have anything to do with it. It's about being good. I thought you were good."

Her words cut me. The door suddenly feels unsteady against my back. I want to sit down, to lower myself to the floor, but I don't. "I am a good man," I say uncertainly.

"No you're not," Julie replies. "Not anymore."

Now I don't say anything.

"She's married, Dad. She's a married woman. She's married to someone you know, someone who's family, someone who helps you out and helps me and he doesn't deserve this. No matter what you tell me, I know that's true. I know Uncle Dave doesn't deserve to be treated this way by you two."

Those last three words are spoken with such hate that the air is sucked out of me.

It takes me a moment to respond. "Julie."

I don't know what else to say. Something inside me is threatening to come loose, some emotion I hadn't expected is rising to the surface.

"Can I be alone?" she asks.

I want to say something else, but there's nothing left.

CHAPTER 45

Switch and I drive home and find Lucy and Moira sitting at my kitchen table. Lucy has a bottle of water sitting on the table in front of her, Moira, one of my Guinness beers.

"What were you thinking?" Moira asks as I walk in. "Going to the hospital that night? Do you realize what would have happened if you'd been caught? What the Judge would've done to make sure you didn't talk?"

"You went to the hospital?" Lucy turns to Switch. "I thought you said he had meetings."

"Huh?" Switch asks.

I turn to Moira. "I thought you could keep a secret."

"Not for something stupid like that. These two need to know when you're doing dumb stuff."

Lucy's stare unnerves me.

"I shouldn't have lied," I tell them. "I'm sorry, but I felt like this was something I had to do. And I didn't want to involve Switch, so I lied to her."

"I see that," Lucy says, and her voice is quiet and direct.

"Look, I didn't do it," I tell them. "He's still alive." I pull out a chair and sit.

Moira clearly doesn't care. "Even if you had," she goes on, "you're not a pro. You would have left evidence. If the Judge catches wind that you're doing something that can bring attention to him, you'll end up swinging from a wooden beam somewhere."

"You'll end up swinging if you lie to me or my sister again," Lucy says.

"I won't. And the Judge is the one who let that agent live."

"He didn't let him live," Lucy says. "He escaped."

"How'd he escape when he was in a coma?" I look around. "And where did Switch go?" I hadn't even seen her leave.

"Someone got him out. And my sister is probably upstairs playing with your rabbit."

"How'd he get out?"

"After that agent was loaded in the car, someone came out of the shadows with a gun and a mask. Kept Daniel at bay, took the keys, and drove off."

"It was someone from the Eastmen," Moira says. "They were watching us, saw what happened, and dumped that agent at the hospital so the cops would come down on us."

"Or it was a traitor," Lucy puts in. "Someone working against us."

"The only other person there was Daniel," I say.

"Doesn't mean it had to be someone there," Moira replies. "Just someone who knew what was happening."

We lapse into silence.

"So," I ask, after a few moments, "what's going to happen to the agent in the hospital?"

"We're going to find a way to get him," Lucy replies.

Switch walks into the room holding Bananas in her arms. She sets him down in my lap. "Thanks," I tell her.

Bananas is tense, as if he's about to jump off at any moment. I stroke his long ears to calm him.

"You look nervous," Lucy says.

"I almost killed a man," I respond. "I'm still a little jittery."

Lucy doesn't get sarcasm. "Listen," she tells me, "we thought you were working with the feds. You weren't, and you proved your innocence. Now all you have to do is lie low and wait for this to end." She looks over at her sister, sitting on the counter and swinging her legs. "Anything that happens to you is going to be because of something you did. So don't do anything."

Moira takes a long drink from her beer.

"So you trust me now?" I ask. "What changed from last night?"

"The only person I trust is my sister," Lucy says, and Switch beams. "But if you stay straight, I won't have a reason to come after you."

"That's comforting."

"So what's next?" Moira asks.

"Next," Lucy says, "we wait and see what the Judge wants us to do."

"Why do you work for him?" I ask. "I get why you worked for Mack, because he found you and helped you, but Mack was always around. I've never seen the Judge. I'm starting to wonder if he even exists, or if he's really just one of you and you're fucking with me."

"We're not fucking with you," Lucy says.

"But has he done anything for you? Has he ever helped you, the way you say Mack did? It seems like all he does is tell you what to do."

"That's what a soldier does."

"You're not a soldier," I tell her, "any more than I am. And I was actually in the army, for about a minute."

"I'm not?" Lucy asks. "Seems like there's not much difference. I kill for a paycheck and do what I'm told. I even keep my head shaved."

"Soldiers fight for honor."

Lucy smiles. "They fight for people," she tells me and then says, "You'll never meet who we fight for. But he does exist."

"You mean the Judge?" I turn toward Moira, who has been quiet throughout this conversation. "Have you ever met him, other than what your dad told you?"

"No," she says, quietly. "But I do believe he's out there."

Lucy stands. "I need to pee." She walks out of the kitchen, toward the stairs.

Switch exclaims, "Me too!" She grabs the rabbit off my lap and hurries after her sister.

I hear Switch rush up the stairs, and then Moira leans over to me and whispers in my ear, "I know about Garrett and Peterson."

I almost pull a muscle trying to hide my surprise. "I don't know what you're talking about."

Moira glances into the hallway. "Shut up and trust me," she whispers. "It's time to tell you the truth."

Realization dawns.

"You're with the FBI," I tell her.

Moira shakes her head. "No one's with the FBI. Not me, and not Garrett or Peterson. We're with the Eastmen."

CHAPTER 46

I wake up the next morning a half hour before I need to, surprised I slept through the night. I take a quick shower and throw on jeans and a sweatshirt. I brush my teeth and that's when my phone vibrates on the side of the sink.

A message from Moira. *Here.*

I spit out toothpaste, dry my mouth, and head to the bedroom window. Moira is leaning against her BMW sedan, arms crossed over her chest, wearing jeans, a brown turtleneck, and an orange vest. She looks up when I look down. A car is parked behind her, but the windows are too tinted to see inside.

I close the curtain, walk to my nightstand, and grab my Glock.

A knock on the bedroom door. I shove the gun into the holster in the back of my pants, cover it with my sweater, and turn as Lucy walks in.

"Moira's here with some guy who works with the Judge," she tells me. "But there's something I need to talk to you about before you take off."

"Okay."

"I want Julie to move back here."

"What? No."

"She's safe with me and Switch." Lucy looks uncomfortable and says, her voice low, "I have a weird feeling some shit is going to go down."

"The answer is no." My phone vibrates again, and I slide it into my pocket.

Lucy grabs my arm. "Tom, please think about it."

I shake her hand off and leave the bedroom, head down the stairs and outside. Moira is still leaning against her silver BMW, hands in her vest pockets.

She opens the driver's side door and climbs inside. "Get in."

We drive off. I don't know where we're going. The car that had been waiting behind Moira veers away.

"I thought about it last night," I tell her, as we head out of Federal Hill and deeper into the city, "and this doesn't make any sense. Why would that guy from the Eastmen have attacked you? The one Lucy tortured?"

"He wasn't attacking me," Moira replies. "He was meeting me, until you interrupted us. And he kept quiet. He died without giving up a name."

"Is that why you told me not to kill Peterson? Because he's working with you?"

"Yes, but also because your plan was really stupid."

"So Garrett and Peterson sent me to the funeral to meet you?"

She glances into her rearview mirror. "That's right."

"But how did they find me?"

"You left your gun in my dad's shop. They tracked you down by the serial number."

"Oh." Knew it.

"See that little street on the right?" Moira points. "Once we turn down it, do what I do."

"What are you going to do?"

Moira ignores me and swerves into the side street. A large truck pulls up behind us and another car, heading in the opposite direction, stops next to us. Doors on the other car pop open and I reach for my Glock, but Moira glances at me, shakes her head, and steps outside. I leave my gun holstered and do the same. Two men wearing thick brown coats, low caps, and jeans are in the other car, the same type of silver BMW Moira drives, and they climb into the car we were using. I follow Moira and slip into the passenger seat.

The truck finishes passing the opening. We drive out, make a hard left, and continue on our way.

"Listen," Moira continues, as if nothing happened, "the Eastmen had been watching my dad for a while, waiting to make a move. They wanted the Judge too, and they knew the Judge would come up here if they took out Mack."

"So you're working with the same people who had your father killed?"

Her expression darkens. "He stopped being my father after he had the Judge kill Freddy."

"You wanted that."

The hand not steering lightly touches my arm. "I lied to you, but that's the only time I did. Freddy did hit me that night, but I *never* asked my father to look into it. Trust me, that was a move he made on his own. And it's something I'll never forget, and never forgive."

Moira turns down another side street, takes the corner quickly, and doubles back. We drive in silence for ten or fifteen minutes and I wonder who to believe.

"Why would the Eastmen want my help?" I ask. "Why would Garrett and Peterson talk to me about getting into Mack's group? I'm just some guy."

"I told you that I only lied to you one time. I was being honest when I said you're the only person I can trust. We weren't going to be able to turn anyone else working with my dad or the Judge."

"What about you? You're a lot closer to Mack's operation than I am."

"My father stopped trusting me after Freddy. The Judge never did. We needed someone who could get inside, someone already working with them. You're it."

"You really had your own father killed?"

"They paid me."

"That makes it worse."

"I would have done it for free, but I wanted them to trust me. Men won't trust anything based only in emotion." Moira glances at me before turning down another side street. "My father was a monster, Tom."

She pulls to a stop. I hadn't paid attention to where we were driving and I'm not sure what neighborhood we're in. The street is a line of shuttered row houses, silent and lifeless, like a line of tombstones.

"If you want the rest of the answers," Moira says, "here's where you'll get them."

CHAPTER 47

They live in an abandoned row house?" I ask.

"No one lives here. This is just where we're meeting." Moira pushes open her door. "Come on inside."

I follow her to the building and notice another car parked about a block away. Other than that, the street is deserted.

"That car up there," I ask her. "Is it with the Eastmen, too?"

"Yes," Moira says, without looking.

She knocks on the plywood that's standing in for a door. It slides over. She steps into the darkness.

I stay outside.

"You have to trust me, Tom," Moira says. "I don't have any reason to bring you here, except to tell you the truth." She pauses. "I could have had you killed about six different times so far."

Fair enough. I follow her in.

She stops as the plywood is pushed back over the opening. My eyes adjust to the dark.

I make out shapes on the floor, two men sitting

down. They hold handguns, and their handguns are pointed at me. To my right is a man with a shotgun.

Moira walks past all of them.

Again, I follow her.

We enter a narrow dark hallway that smells like cigarettes. More men stand in here, maybe four or five, leaning against the walls. One says something I don't catch. The others laugh.

A staircase is at the opposite end. A man is sitting on the bottom step, but he looks up at us and laboriously climbs to his feet. He lets Moira pass but stops me.

"Out," the man says.

"What?"

"Out."

I look at Moira. "I think he wants me to leave."

"He means put your arms out," she says.

I lift my arms and he pats me down. He doesn't seem surprised to find my gun. He slips it into his jacket pocket.

Moira and I walk up the creaky beaten stairs and into a hall that splits left and right. Every door is closed. Moira walks to the second door on the left, knocks, and steps away.

"You're not going in with me?" I ask.

"House rules," Moira tells me. "They only let one person in the room at a time."

"Why?"

"Come on in, Tom," a man's voice says from the other side of the door.

There's that fear, that old panic, the urge to run down the stairs and out of this house and find Julie and run away, but I know I can't leave. Not until I'm allowed to go, and that won't happen until I've met with whoever is waiting inside this room.

Moira touches my hand.

"Trust me," she says.

I step inside.

The room is bare and decrepit with walls that look like they've been chewed in the corners, dirt on the floor, dim light from a dusty window. A man sits at the far end of the room on a metal folding chair.

He stands and he's taller than I am, six three or six four. His dark hair is shaved close and he looks young but not too young, maybe just under forty. His eyes are blue. I can see a muscular frame underneath his black T-shirt and blue jeans.

The door shuts behind me.

"Hi, Tom," he says, and his voice is coarse, his throat lined with sandpaper. "My name's Wallace. I heard you visited our man at the hospital. Finishing the job?"

Wallace's blue eyes bore into me.

"He and Garrett had been talking to me," I answer. "I thought they were with the FBI. I wanted to find out the truth."

"They were never in the FBI. To be honest, we were all surprised you fell for that. But they are partners. Garrett's at the hospital right now, guarding Peterson."

I can't believe I fell for it either, but hope shrouds everything, even lies. I hadn't realized how much I wanted help.

"You should know," Wallace says, "there's no cavalry coming. There's no one from the FBI looking out for you and your daughter. There's no one to turn to."

"I know."

"The Judge probably said he could keep you safe. He can't."

"I know that too."

"You saw the men we have downstairs. You think the Judge's people could stop us?"

I tell Wallace what I think he wants to hear: "No."

Wallace looks at me until I speak again.

"I'll tell you the same thing I told the Judge's people. I don't want to be involved. I just want to be left alone."

"I'm not what you think." Wallace's face loses the tension. "Those men downstairs? They respect me, but it's not out of fear. The Judge rules by fear. That's not me. I'm not going to lie to you, and I'm not going to hurt you. From what I can tell, and from what Moira told me, you're a good man, an innocent man. A caring dad. You don't deserve to be in this mess."

I stay silent.

Wallace brings his hands together, rubs them. "I need your help, just like Moira and Garrett and Peterson told you. We need as many eyes and ears as close to the Judge's people as we can get. This is a war, and I need to know as much as I can about the Judge to keep my people safe. Moira helps, but you're the one living with the Judge's two best hit men. I could use your help."

"I'm not sure what you want me to do."

"I want to draw out the Judge. If we can find him, then we can end this quick. I can get most of his men, but not him." He stops speaking for a moment and studies me. "I'm going to tell you something, and it's not something I need to share. But I want you to know I trust you."

Wallace pauses again.

"We're going to attack in two days."

"What does that mean?"

"It means that, in two days, we're going to kill all of his people."

Lucy and Switch flash through my mind. "They all have to die?"

Wallace nods. "You have to understand, Mack went after a certain type. Young men and women he could brainwash and control. And he did a good job of it. They were loyal to him and now that he's dead, they're loyal to the Judge. Beaten and brainwashed, and too loyal to be saved."

"It seems like you and the Judge want the same thing. Lots of death."

"He and I are past the point where we can turn away from that."

"Moira told me Mack killed your son, and tried to kill you."

Wallace's expression changes and I recognize the look, the loss of composure, the hollowness behind his eyes. It takes him a moment to recover, but he does recover. "Yeah," he says. "That's right."

"And now Mack's dead. Everyone else is irrelevant."

"Everyone else is a soldier," Wallace corrects me.

This time I don't argue the term. "Soldiers can be given orders to stop fighting."

"They can, but that's not what the Judge is telling them to do. Even with the Judge dead, they won't stop. As much as we like to say soldiers fight for causes, they fight for people. And they'll die fighting for Mack."

Wallace walks over to a boarded-up window and pulls a loose piece of wood. He lets it slap back into place.

"There's going to be a lot of death," he tells me. "But afterward, you and Julie will be free. Free from them, free from us, free from all of this. And that's what you want, right?"

"Yes."

He stops picking at the board and stares into me. "What else do you want?"

"I want my life the way it was before I ever got in touch with Mack and his people." I'm surprised by my honesty.

"We can't go back, Tom," Wallace tells me. "That land is dead and salted. You're standing on it, hoping it grows around you again, and that will never happen. All we can do is move forward, find somewhere new to go." He walks back to the chair and leans over it. "I'll take you there. I promise you. But I need your help. And you, more than most, know why I'm so driven."

"You know what happened to me?"

He nods.

"I already know I'll never get my wife back," I say.

"And my son will never return," Wallace replies. "But I can't stare into the void and do nothing. I have to scream."

Silence. I let it persist while I weigh my options.

I can't go to the cops without admitting my own crimes and, even worse, risking the wrath of the Judge or Wallace. And that wrath could come down on anyone I care about.

I can't run without eventually being tracked down, or the risk of being found forever hanging over my head. I'd spent three years worried that Mack would break our deal and kill me, fake reporter or not. I need that worry to end.

I have no idea who's going to win this crime war, but I can't trust that whoever wins has any real desire to keep me alive. I'm a loose end, and these people cut off loose ends.

The only thing to do is double-cross everyone without being discovered. Steer these groups into a bloody battle and hope they slaughter each other. Or leave them so broken that they're no longer a threat.

Sometimes the antidote is poison.

"What do you need me to do?" I ask.

CHAPTER 48

Daniel

I wait for the taps on the wall and, when I hear them, I hurry to my feet and brush myself off, but quickly, because this fucking abandoned crackhouse we're holed up in is colder than Prancer's balls. I had to sit huddled on the floor with my knees buried in my chest and my chin tucked down like I'm having withdrawals just to keep warm. I open the door and look down the hall and there's no one there but I can hear Moira and that nerd heading down the stairs. I step out and walk into Wallace's room.

He's standing behind this gray metal chair and leaning on it with both hands. He looks like he could snap it in half but it also kind of looks like it's holding him up. All depends on his expression, I guess. Right now I can't read nothing.

"You trust him?" Wallace asks me.

"That Tom guy?" I shrug and slide my hands into my pockets so I don't have to think of something for my hands to do while Wallace is slowly freezing me with that icy stare. "I guess. I don't really know. What does it matter?"

"It matters because I told him that we're going to attack in two days," he says, and his voice is all thoughtful.

"Why'd you do that?"

"Because, for the time being, I need his trust. And this was for nothing if he goes home and tells the twins about us."

"I don't know if I'd trust him," I say, honestly. "But you're not staying here, right?"

"The men downstairs are already leaving," Wallace tells me. He lets go of the chair and reaches down and scratches his ankle. It's not really a tough guy thing to do but I guess everyone sometimes has an itchy ankle.

"Are you listening?" Wallace asks.

Shit he was talking. "I didn't get that last part," I tell him.

Wallace gets that same disappointed look that Mack used to get in his eyes but at least he's not a dick about it like Mack was because Wallace blinks and the look is gone. "We only need him because he can deliver the twins. Once we have them, we won't need him any longer."

I nod and wonder what any of this has to do with me. Maybe Wallace just wants to try out ideas with me, like some kind of war counsel. That's a nice idea even though I'm definitely wrong.

"What about that reporter?" I ask. "Supposedly there's some reporter who he keeps feeding information to, in case anything happens to him. And now he's seen you, so he's definitely going to let the reporter know what you look like."

Wallace folds his arms across his chest. "That's why you're here," he tells me.

"Okay," I say, and I nod and I wonder if he'd care if I pulled out a cigarette.

Wallace looks at me curiously. "Why are you nodding? I haven't told you what I wanted."

I stop nodding. "Right. Sorry."

I really want a cigarette.

CHAPTER 49

Tom

I get home and find Switch staring intensely into her right palm and Lucy sitting on the couch. They're watching a show about rich married women living in New York.

Neither of them acknowledges me.

I head upstairs and close my bedroom door. Then I walk into the bathroom and lean over the sink. My elbows press hard into the cold granite. My chest aches and I place my palm on the center of my ribs, the way you apply pressure to calm a wound.

I sit on the closed toilet seat and close my eyes. I can't calm down.

I'm getting used to being afraid but it's never consumed me. And this is more than fear, it's anxiety—anxiety about delving even deeper into these groups, instead of running away or turning myself into the cops.

I want to confess.

But I don't have anyone to turn to. I thought this entire time that the FBI was on my side, that they knew and would forgive my sins. But there's no one there, no one but criminals and killers.

So I don't have a choice.

To keep the people I care about safe, I have to go deeper.

I uncurl out of the little ball I've tucked myself in, stand, and lean heavily on the sink. I look at myself in the mirror and the fear on my face startles me. In fact, I'm so shocked that I feel the panic return. Again that urge to turn to someone, to beg for help, rushes over me.

Ruth. For a second, she's the answer. Confessing to Ruth would bring my secret to life, and Ruth is one of the only honest things in my life. But Ruth—no, she can never know. Dave? He's a high-powered attorney with lots of connections. Hope suddenly rises in me, but Dave is a high-powered *real estate* attorney. The chances that he can help with this are small. Really, there's no chance.

Friends at the school, fellow teachers, family outside the state, no one comes to mind. I'm alone.

I have to go deeper. Go deeper until this war is over, until my daughter and I are free from threats. And then leave this city. Depart from this life.

I open the door and Julie and Lucy are waiting in my bedroom. Julie is standing at the door, her arms crossed impatiently. Switch sits on the edge of my bed.

"What are you doing here?" I ask. "You're supposed to be with Ruth."

"I needed to get some different clothes. What were you doing? You've been in there forever."

"You okay?" Lucy asks, her dark eyes intense.

I nod.

"Can we go to Patterson Park?" Julie asks. "Switch has never been, and I was telling her how you, me, and Mom used to go."

"Who's we?"

"All of us."

Lucy shrugs. "Should be fine." She catches my eye and gives me a barely perceptible nod.

I don't like the idea, but I know from my conversation with Wallace that the attack won't happen today. Today, at least, we're safe.

"Okay," I decide. "Sure."

૮ͻ૮ͻ

The park is only about a twenty-minute drive from Federal Hill, which is good because my small truck doesn't have a backseat and the four of us are cramped in the cab. I pull into a space on Patterson Park Avenue and we tumble out and stretch.

"It's cold," Julie comments, and she zips her jacket.

I close my coat. Switch and Lucy leave theirs open.

"What's that?" Switch asks.

"It's a Pagoda," I answer. "It's Japanese."

"What's it doing in the middle of a city?" Switch exclaims. "That's silly!"

"Well," I tell her, "I've actually never known why it's here. Let's find out."

"The more you know," she says.

We walk over to the Pagoda. It's a red and yellow cylindrical four-story structure. Railways guard three landings and a roof that looks like a painstakingly-crafted umbrella. Curiously, the ornamental building isn't out of place here, in the middle of this blue-collar neighborhood, in this park where prostitutes and dealers used to dwell. It brings a sense of tranquil peace, the way any solemn monument does.

Julie is practically skipping ahead of us. She was in a

good mood on the ride over, talkative and chirpy, playfully pushing into me or the twins whenever my truck turned. Then I spot Anthony waiting at the Pagoda, slouched against one of the old green cannons adjacent to it.

Julie runs up and hugs him.

"Did you know he was going to be here?" I ask Lucy.

"Nope."

Anthony walks over to us, one hand around Julie's shoulders. She's leaning into him so forcefully it looks like they're in a three-legged race.

"Hi, Mister Starks," Anthony says. I notice he's switched from calling me Tom.

"Anthony. I should have known."

He looks at Julie in surprise. "You didn't tell your dad I was coming?"

"No, but it's fine," she assures him. "I wanted you to meet Lucy and Switch, but I guess they had something to do."

I turn and the twins are gone. I hadn't even realized they'd left. I look around and see them walking toward a group of trees.

"You'll meet them later," Julie tells Anthony. "Dad, is it okay if Anthony and I walk around for a bit and meet you back here in an hour?"

"One hour," I reply. "It's cold."

"Are you sure that's okay with you, Mister Starks?" Anthony asks.

"That's fine." I can't tell if he's being a smartass.

They walk off. I follow the twins to the trees.

It's been years since I've been back at Patterson Park.

The memories make me too sad to return. Like Julie said, we used to come here with Renee and sit on the long grassy slopes and watch people walk their dogs or play softball or touch football. I've fallen in love with Renee here, proposed to her next to the Pagoda, and when I decided to get revenge for her death, I came here the night before.

I walk down a sloped sidewalk and over to the sisters, shadowy figures in a grove of trees.

Lucy is staring into her phone and Switch is doing that weird muttering. I stay to the side, wait for them to finish. After a minute or so, they both turn toward me.

"Probably best that her boyfriend doesn't see us," Lucy says.

I understand. The fewer the number of people that can identify her, the better.

"Anyway, I don't see what the big deal is with this place," Lucy continues.

"Well, she just came here to see Anthony."

"I mean the big deal for you. There's nothing to do here. What did your little family do when you used to come years ago?"

"Not much. Bring food. People watch. Isn't your sister cold?"

Lucy had buttoned up her denim jacket, but Switch left hers open, and only has on a T-shirt underneath.

"She's fine," Lucy says, then presses, "We're just wondering why this park matters."

"I don't know," I tell her honestly. "It's just a nice place to get away. I like places like this, where you're in the middle of the city and it feels like you're miles away. Where it's peaceful."

"Like a cemetery?"

"That's right where your mind goes, huh? But, yeah, kind of like that. Any place where you can find some peace."

"There's always danger," Lucy replies.

"Do you ever relax?"

Lucy gives me a level look. "Sometimes. When I listen to music, I kind of slip into my own world."

"What kind of music?"

"Anything, really. Mostly jazz."

"Really?"

She seems miffed. "Why are you surprised?"

"Renee used to love jazz. She got me into it."

"What'd she like?"

"Billie Holiday, Charlie Parker, Coltrane, Modern Jazz Quartet, all the greats."

Lucy nods. "That was a good woman you had. I love Billie Holiday."

"I can't listen to her anymore."

Something in Lucy's face softens. "Too much?"

"Too much, yeah."

Lucy jerks her head toward Switch. "She never liked her. Said her voice was too scratchy. Didn't like the hitch. I told her that you need to listen to her when you're sad, way down. That's the only way you understand her. You have to meet her at that low point."

"And when you do," I say, "you understand everything."

"She's a torch down there."

Silence.

"Let's walk," she says.

We head out of the grove and onto the long stretch of grass. The cold has made the ground hard underfoot, the grass brittle. The long fields are mostly empty. A dog trots in front of a man a hill away. I don't know where Julie and Anthony are.

"I don't like the book I've been reading," Lucy says, as Switch walks a few feet behind us. "I don't even know why I'm doing it. I never read. Same with TV and movies. I just can't get into them. Seems so fake to me."

I try to say something, but she keeps on talking.

"Music's different. It's real. It matters. You can hear it in their voices." Lucy puts a hand on my arm. "Look."

"What?"

"Over there, against that tree."

Julie and Anthony are kissing, arms wrapped around each other, her head tilted up.

The sight bothers me. Anthony obviously knows I'm at this park, and he's kissing my daughter as if I don't matter.

But there's something else in me, a weird happiness for Julie's happiness, for Julie having the chance to experience teenage passion.

We keep walking. They don't break apart or even seem to realize that we're only twenty or so yards away.

"Listen," I tell Lucy, "I need to know Julie is safe."

Lucy sighs. "I told you she is."

"I mean safe from you. If the Judge told you to kill us, would you?"

I feel those flickers of panic inside and I tighten a fist, trying to keep calm.

"He's not going to have me kill you and Julie. But if he did—" We stop walking and Lucy looks up at me, her dark eyes polluted clouds. "If he did, I'd find a way to protect her."

"What about me?"

"You'll be fucked," Lucy says. Switch giggles. The three of us start walking again.

CHAPTER 50

Julie

Dinners at Ruth's have been *so* awkward ever since I caught my dad and Ruth. I mean, they were awkward before, just because, seriously, it was like she and Dave could barely stand each other sometimes, but now Ruth is totally jumpy and practically gets pale every time I talk.

And yeah, okay. Part of it is my fault. Like tonight, when we're eating some chicken thing Ruth made and I ask, "Have you heard from my dad lately?"

I'm watching Ruth as I say it, and I see her jaw get all hard.

"Not recently," Ruth says.

I try not to smile, and I know I'm being a total asshole about this, but I'm also kind of like *fuck her.*

Dave coughs.

"How's school going?" Ruth asks.

"It's okay," I tell her, even though it's better than okay. I was sort of a shitty student a few years ago, but things switched. I don't know why, but school just got easier. I haven't had anything less than a B for the past two years. Maybe the teachers take it easy on me because they know my mom was murdered.

Damn, I shouldn't have phrased it like that.

I take a drink of water because my throat is suddenly raw.

"Do you have finals?" Dave asks.

"In a couple of classes. Other classes, they want me to write a paper or something."

He nods. I pick at my chicken even though my appetite is gone. Dinner goes on, and Dave and Ruth still ignore each other. They both just talk to me.

Must be lonely.

This is all getting really fucking sad so I excuse myself, leave them to their silence, and head upstairs. I actually have homework to do, but instead I pull out this book Lucy gave me to read, *Her Deadly Catch*. It's okay, I guess. Kind of predictable. An FBI agent falls in love with a serial killer or something, and it sort of reminds me of *Twilight*. Everyone is beautiful and sort of perfect. But reading it now, after thinking about what happened to my mom...I don't know. Too much is missing in that book for me to care.

There's no real pain.

I close the book, text Anthony and tell him it was nice seeing him, and I go to bed early.

Christ. I'm too young to be depressed.

CHAPTER 51

Tom

"It's like none of these people wanted to kill, not really," Grant says the following afternoon.

"You say that, but they all did," Ashley counters. "Even if they were reluctant, they still did."

"But they *had* to," Grant argues back. "It was war. There's necessity, and then there's excess. And even the other guy, Berrendo, knew what he did was excessive."

The class is discussing El Sordo's last stand in *For Whom the Bell Tolls*. Neither of the twins is with me. For better or worse, I guess I'm earning their trust.

And not having them around has settled my jumpy nerves. A weird deep calm has filled me after my panic attack yesterday. The knowledge that, tomorrow, this will all be over.

"But wasn't the violence necessary?" I ask. "Berrendo needed proof that they were dead."

Grant looks into his book before he answers. Funny how students have no problems debating their peers, but are more cautious with their professors. This debate is largely subjective and, truthfully, neither Grant nor Ashley is wrong.

"I feel like he could have gotten the proof some different way," Grant says, still staring into the book. "Other than cutting off their heads."

"It's not like they had fingerprinting back then," Kendra puts in, and then she glances at me. "They didn't, right?"

"They had fingerprinting," I say. "But I'm not sure of its availability during the Spanish Civil War. I think you're debating something deeper, though. Hemingway's characters kill frequently in this book but, when you go inside their heads, they all have reasons, and the need to justify those reasons."

"It's weird," Kendra remarks. "They do these terrible acts, but they seem more emotional about it than people nowadays."

"Maybe it's just this country," Ashley replies. "Everyone says we're desensitized. Too much violence on television, too many guns in people's hands."

"Right," Grant says. "Because the thing that will stop gun violence is less guns to protect ourselves."

"I like your first point," I quickly put in, to make sure the discussion doesn't turn into a never-ending one on guns and violence in America. "I think the attitude of these characters goes beyond violence. It has to do with seeing your own homeland slaughtered. It makes a chasm in a country, and in its people."

"What do you mean?" Grant asks.

"Well, we've had plenty of wars, and suffered loss, but we haven't had battles in this country since the Civil War. And I think the sight of bombed buildings and widespread devastation changes people. Makes it person-

al. Especially when you're fighting your own country-
men. You can't help but be changed."

The students start to pack up. "Finish the book for
next time," I call out, and I turn off my laptop as they file
out.

"So I was wondering?" a voice asks a few moments
later. "Do you want my apple?"

Ruth is standing in the doorway.

"What are you doing here?"

She walks up to me and kisses me lightly on the lips.
"I thought about what we talked about, about choosing to
be together. And I have an idea."

So much has happened since our meeting in the parking garage that I haven't given our conversation much
thought.

"Okay."

"My big idea," she says, "is to do nothing."

"I don't understand."

Ruth steps away, walks over to one of the desks, and
runs her fingers over the wood. "I don't want this to end.
But I can't run off."

"I don't think I can either."

"So let's not change anything. Let's just keep doing
what we're doing." Ruth walks back to me. "Why do we
have to stop?"

Her lips find mine.

Then they break away.

"You can't, can you?" I ask.

She shakes her head.

"This is the only wrong thing I've ever done in my
life," Ruth says then recants. "Not the only thing, but the
worst thing. But it doesn't even feel wrong, not all the
time." Her jaw sets in the hard way I've grown to recognize when she's angry. "I hate that we have to play by
these rules. I can't leave Dave and I can't be with you.

And even if I could leave Dave, would you want me to? After we spoke that last time, didn't everything seem more real? And scary?" I nod. Her face relaxes. "I'm glad it's not just me."

"The thing is," I tell her, "time apart might be for the best. I have a lot happening right now."

"Is it stuff with work?" Ruth presses. "Or Julie?"

I can't tell her the truth. Of course I can't. "It's work."

"I'm here for you," Ruth says.

Someone coughs.

Ruth and I break away from each other. I turn toward the doorway expecting to see Dave. Instead it's Moira.

She watches us with a thin smile.

Ruth glances at me. "Who's she?"

"One of my students," I lie. "She needs to talk with me about a project."

"It's okay," Ruth says. "I'll go." She gathers her purse and heads out. Moira doesn't move aside, and Ruth has to slide sideways to pass her.

"She didn't have to leave," Moira says.

"Shut up."

Moira closes the door behind her, walks over to me, and sits in one of the desks in the front row. "Banging your sister-in-law, Tom? Your married sister-in-law. I'm surprised."

"What are you doing here, Moira?"

She frowns. "That's not the way you should talk to the person who's going to save your life."

"*Might* save my life."

"Come on, Tom. I'm fucking with you." Moira crosses her legs underneath the desk and scratches her ankle. "I always thought college teachers slept with their students."

"I only have time to teach my students one thing at a time."

Moira laughs.

"Since you know about Ruth," I tell her, "then you have to do something for me. In addition to me and Julie, I want safety extended to Ruth."

She frowns. "I'm not here to negotiate."

"And her husband."

"Aren't you noble?"

"These people are important to me."

Moira taps her finger on the desk. "Chances are no one cares about your little fuck-toy and her husband. Or even knows about them."

"You knew about them. You knew exactly who she was."

Those long legs uncross. Moira stands. "Fine, I'll tell Wallace. But you have to do something for us, and it's the reason I'm here. Everything goes down tomorrow. And we need you to deliver Switch to the Eastmen."

CHAPTER 52

Daniel

I hide behind the door and try like hell not to shut my eyes and I pray to whoever is up there listening that Lucy doesn't come into Tom's bedroom while I'm in here looking around. I just heard her and her batshit sister on the other side of the door in the hall having a conversation or as close as they come to having a conversation, mainly just Lucy talking about someone named Charlie Parker—and I'd heard the name before so maybe he used to be president or something?—and Switch saying her usual "I dunno."

Their voices come closer and closer and I start to panic because the house was empty and I thought I had enough time to go through it but the downstairs door opened and I was trapped. I take out my gun and I tell myself I'm about to pull open the door and start shooting when the voices are gone.

Are they waiting?

Did they hear me?

Do they know I'm here?

My god, I will inject and inhale and smoke and snort every drug that's ever been made if I can just get out of this if I can have one more day. I'm not doing good, that's for sure, not good at all, and I'd spent most of the time as we get closer to tomorrow stuck in a hazy world of Xanax and beer and pot, trying to have a hardness that just isn't me. I can't believe I haven't been caught yet and I expect to, expect to be called in to the Judge and have someone force me to my knees and run a knife across my neck, like I'd seen happen once and I'd been so sick that I'd gone home and thrown up everything that had ever been inside me.

Still no sounds from the other side and my gun is sweaty in my hand. I press my ear against the door and listen as hard as I can and suddenly I do hear something, the bright exploding cheerful sound of a TV being turned on and I know the twins have gone downstairs. I can't go out the front door but I hadn't come in that way anyway. Instead, I go to the kid's room and slide her window back open and dangle off the ledge and drop to the ground. Even with Switch and Lucy here, kids are still dumb enough to leave their windows unlocked, back when I was boosting electronics you could always count on a teen to leave their window open. I climb over the back-yard fence and make my way down the narrow little street to my car and call Wallace and tell him that, no, I haven't found anything about a reporter in Tom's class-room or his sister-in-laws' place or his house.

◌∕◌◌∕◌

Next and last stop of the day and then I can go home to my apartment and annihilate myself. I head through Hampden and stop at the little U of a street where Moira lives and I'm happy to be doing something that doesn't revolve around some nerd teacher at a bullshit community college. Actually I don't know why Moira wants to see me but I'm pretty sure it's for something important and it makes me feel good to be with Moira. It's not only because I've rubbed my dick raw ever since I first saw her, although that was nice, it's because she's in this the same way I am and she's so relaxed and chill that it has the same effect on me. She's the best drug, a delicious soul-satisfying drop that delves deeper than anything else and touches me in places no other drug ever has or will.

"Oh, hey," Moira says when she opens the door and sees me standing there. "I just got back from the college."

She doesn't feel the same about me. I'm okay with that.

I'm okay with that because she turns and walks into her house and I get to see her walk away, the curvy loopy W of her ass cheeks swinging a little and I just barely manage to pull my eyes back up when she turns around.

"What are you doing?" she snaps. "Come in and close the door."

"Okay," I say and I do, although I don't know why she's being paranoid because we're both on the same two teams and anyone who saw us together, if they're from the Judge or from the Eastmen, wouldn't have a reason to suspect anything. Not like when Wallace makes me drive him around neighborhoods everywhere, like he's using my life to prove some point.

"What's up?" I ask. I step inside and into the smell of some type of lovely scented candle. I can't identify the smell exactly, just that it smells red.

"I want you to pull up to my car with yours, open the trunk and take the machine gun. It needs to go back to Wallace."

"Why don't I just take it back to the shed myself?"

We all call it the shed but really it's an underground storage unit survivor thing where Mack kept all of the guns that I guess were too illegal for him to keep at the store.

"Because I don't want someone to follow you there," Moira says, and her lips get thick like waves and I see myself riding those waves and forget what's going on.

"What?" I ask.

"Did you change the lock on the shed? Did you remember to do that?"

I think hard and can't remember can't think of anything now but those red lips in front of me, the kind of lips that you want to trace with your finger your tongue.

"Sure."

Moira looks doubtfully at me.

I smile confidently at her.

"What are you doing?" she asks. "You look like a jack-o-lantern."

I give up smiling both because Moira asked me to and because I feel sweat trickling down my right armpit and I don't know if I already have a stain and I can't check because Moira is looking at me. I fold my arms across my chest and wish that pose looked tougher than it does but it's hard to look tough when you're one hundred and thirty pounds and your arms have so little definition they look like long wrists.

Moira gives me a weird look and a quick shake of her head. "Are you ready for tomorrow?"

This is a perfect question to ask when I'm in my tough-guy pose and I tell her, "Yeah, sure."

"Are you really ready?" she asks.

"Yeah, sure."

"Are you ready to kill if you have to?" Moira keeps talking before I can say *yeah sure*. "You never have, right? You might not be able to let someone do it for you."

I'm about to protest but she steps toward me and touches my arm. "I know you have it in you," she says.

Much of me is melting and it's like winds swirling through my heart at her touch. There's no doubt now, there's no uncertainty, there's nothing but those swirling winds and the waves of her lips and the soft lines that are too lazy to run straight down either side of her body and the toss of her black hair and the loss inside me the hole that no drug, no food, no drink, no god, no man, no heaven, nothing but a woman can fill. And I tell her yeah sure no problem when the time comes I'll pull the trigger. And her hand leaves my arm. I feel it later long after.

CHAPTER 53

Tom

I muddle my way through two comp classes and head home. I drive slowly, thinking about what Moira has asked me to do. She told me she'd text me the location tomorrow morning, but I don't know how I'm going to deliver Switch wherever Moira wants me to take her. And the fact that Peterson is still breathing has changed my mindset. I'd been willing to kill before, but now I'm not so sure. I feel like I've been given a reprieve.

Switch and Lucy are wolfing down Taco Bell at my kitchen table. I perch on a bar stool at the counter and watch them.

Lucy glances over at me. "We got you some," she says.

"You did?"

She holds out a bag. "Hungry?"

"Sure." I take the bag, unwrap a taco, and bite into it.

"How's it taste?" Lucy asks.

"Like shame, but I don't really care. Thanks for getting me something to eat."

"It's the least we can do," Lucy replies, "since you're letting us stay with you."

That sounds like I had a choice, but I let it go.

"So, Tom," Lucy asks, "you like teaching?"

I nod, but the nod turns into a shrug. "It's okay. Why? Thinking about switching fields?"

Lucy wipes her mouth with a napkin. Switch uses the back of her arm. "No way," Lucy says. "I hate being in front of crowds."

I'm about to take another bite, but that comment stops me. "Really?"

"Why are you surprised?"

"I'm surprised you're scared of anything, with what you do."

Lucy finishes off what's left of her taco and swallows. "I'm still a person. Can I ask you something else?"

"Sure."

Lucy stands, picks up her chair, turns it toward me, and sits back down. She rests her elbows across the top and stares at me with her dark intense eyes. "Did you find out who killed your wife?"

"Yes."

"What'd you do to him?"

I shake my head. "Diane killed him. They killed each other in front of me." I decide not to mention how I finished them off.

"Not him. I know about that. I'm talking about the guy who ordered it."

"I found him too."

"What'd you do?"

"I let him go."

"Let him off with a warning?" Lucy asks with a smile.

Switch jumps to her feet and shakes her finger at an

imaginary person to her right. "Don't you kill my wife again!"

She collapses back in her chair and the twins laugh for a bit. "Why'd you let him go?" Lucy asks when they're finished.

I remember the parking garage in Boston where I'd found him, where I cornered him, where I forced him to confess. Philip Stone had been a lawyer that Renee dated, loved, and lost. He married someone else but he still saw Renee and, eventually, impregnated her. Renee raised Julie on her own and ended things with Philip, except for one last fling. This fling happened when she and I were married, and the guilt consumed Renee to the verge of confessing to me and to Philip's family. Desperate to keep his marriage intact, Philip had Renee killed. And after learning all this, despite my anger, I couldn't kill Julie's biological father. I don't know if I can ever tell Julie who he was, but I can't kill him.

"I didn't have it in me," I say.

"You had it in you the other night," Lucy counters, "when you smashed that man into a coma."

"It's not that I couldn't kill him," I amend. "I didn't want to." I hope Lucy doesn't notice that I'm avoiding looking at Switch.

But her thoughts are elsewhere. "You know?" Lucy muses. "I've never actually wanted to kill anyone. Except my dad."

"How many people have you killed?"

"I told you before," she says. "No reason to count those numbers. What good can come from knowing?"

"I guess that's true."

We sit in silence. Switch stands, gathers the wrappers from the food, and throws them away.

"Do you two," I ask, "ever date?"

Lucy looks horrified and Switch bursts out laughing. "Each other?"

"What? No. Other people."

The horrified look passes. "Again," Lucy says, "what good can come from it? With what we do?"

"A lot," I say.

Lucy disagrees. "Too risky. And relationships always have a dark side to them. The serious ones are full of secrets."

"Not always."

"Says the guy," Lucy points out, "whose dead wife was cheating on him, and who is currently sleeping with his married sister-in-law."

"I may not be the best example."

"What's going to happen with that?" Lucy asks. "With your sister-in-law?"

"I'm not sure. Probably something bad. There's no way it can end well."

"It can if her husband dies."

"What?" I can't tell if Lucy is serious. "Don't kill him."

Lucy grins. "I'm fucking with you, Tom."

"I don't want anything to happen to Dave. You understand that, right?"

"Come on, Switch. Let's watch TV."

They head out of the kitchen, down the hall.

"I really don't want him hurt," I call out. I head to my bedroom and try to read, but it's hard to concentrate. And impossible to sleep. I spend most of the night awake, waiting for morning and what I have to do to these women.

CHAPTER 54

Morning. It's raining. A memory floats at the edges of my mind but I can't quite capture it—something about winter, and Renee and Julie, and peace. And then it's gone.

Today's the day people die.

I wearily head into the bathroom, wash my face, brush my teeth, throw on some clothes. I look at my phone and read a text from Moira. Then I kneel and, for the first time in years, pray.

I walk downstairs and find Switch sitting in the den, cross-legged on the couch, a bowl of cereal in her lap.

"Where's Lucy?" I ask.

I expect an *I dunno* but instead Switch grins. "She had to do something."

"Any idea what?"

"I dunno."

Something unsettling rises in me, but I force it down.

We stare at the program she's watching, some muted talk show about politics.

"You like this show?" I ask.

"I like watching yelling."

That makes me smile a little. "I knew this woman in your line of work," I tell Switch. "Her name was Diane."

"I knew Diane," Switch says.

"She told me that Mack's people were the weapon of the world. Like killers were the action that came from our private thoughts and emotions."

"I dunno."

We watch the silent program for a bit, and then I ask, "Want to grab lunch?"

"I'm eating now."

"Then come with me while I eat," I tell her. My throat has gone dry. Lucy would have seen right through me. "I know this restaurant," I add. "It's really close by."

"Okay."

∽∾∽

Moira's text read, *Bring Switch to 203 Bar, Fed Hill 11 a.m.*

I write her back, *We're on our way.*

∽∾∽

"The hamburgers are really that good?" Switch asks as we drive down Hanover Street.

"Best in Baltimore." The rain has stopped and left the day gray and icy. My heater is turned up as high as it can go, but I'm still cold.

"I like Julie," Switch says.

"Yeah, she likes you too."

We pull to a stop at a traffic light. The 203 Bar is a block away. I see an SUV parked across from it, and I know that the SUV is filled with men who are going to kidnap Switch, force her to tell them everything she knows about the Judge, and put a bullet in her head.

I use my windshield wipers to swat away the rain and wonder how Julie is doing. She has a sleepover tonight, which works out perfectly. I don't want her anywhere she can be found.

"What were you like as a teenager?" I ask Switch.

"What?"

"What were you like?"

Switch is about to say something but stops. She looks at me and, again, starts to speak but doesn't. She just shakes her head. "I dunno."

The light turns green.

I take a right, turn off Hanover, and onto Randall Street. An angry looking man in a tank top strides past the truck.

"Where are you going?" Switch asks.

"My mistake. Restaurant's closed."

CHAPTER 55

S witch climbs out of my truck when we get back home, but I blurt out that I need to pick up something at the drug store and drive away before she can stop me. I head right back to the bar. The black tinted SUV is still sitting across the street. I park, climb out of my truck, and walk past the Eastmen's vehicle. I don't have the guts to peer inside.

The restaurant is split into two long dark rooms, side-by-side, with televisions mounted on the walls and black plastic taped over the windows. Four men sit at a table by the front door. They glance up as I enter and watch me.

Wallace sits in the back of the other room, at the farthest table away, wearing a suit jacket with no tie and a shirt buttoned underneath it. Moira is perched on the edge of the table and studying her nails, her long bare legs crossed. Otherwise, the restaurant is empty.

One of the men stands, frisks me, and takes my Glock.

Wallace leans back in his chair as I approach and then indicates for me to take the chair opposite him. Moira sighs and slides off the table. She pulls out a chair from the table next to Wallace's.

"Couldn't go through with it?" Wallace asks, his voice mild.

"I'm sorry," I tell him. "I really am. I know you have to kill Switch, but I don't want it to be because of something I did. I can't."

"I like that you showed up here," Wallace says. "Men usually disappear when they let me down. Or they try to. But I'm not surprised. Moira said there was only a fifty-fifty chance you'd actually bring Switch here."

"And I was being generous," she puts in.

I figure now is probably a good time to give them the speech I prepared, the one where I beg for mercy. "I know you're mad at me, but I want to ask you to spare my daughter. She's just a girl, and she doesn't—"

Wallace looks disgusted. "I'd never hurt a kid."

I'm more relieved than I let my expression show. "Thank you." A pause. "What about a thirty-year old man?"

Wallace laughs. "Here's the thing," he says. "This comes down to trust. I have to know I can trust you. You're living with our enemy, and it seems like you've made friends."

"I haven't. I just don't want to kill anyone."

"Everyone is getting killed. Including Switch. We have men at your house right now."

"What?" I push back my chair. The four men who were sitting by the door are now standing behind me.

I look back at Wallace.

"You care a lot about that woman," Moira observes.

"It's not her," I tell them urgently. "My daughter might come home. I keep sending her away and she keeps showing back up. What if something happens to her? Did you think about that?"

"Lower your voice, Tom," Wallace admonishes me. "I told you I'd never let a kid get hurt." He pauses. "But accidents happen."

"What's that mean?" I feel the men move closer.

"It means that, even though my men are professionals, there could be a lot of bullets flying around. You don't always know where they'll land."

"You just said you'd never hurt a child!"

"Not intentionally."

"Look, you have to stop the attack! Please!"

Wallace glances at his watch again. "I only have two minutes."

I take a step toward him and strong hands grip my arms, like steel pressing into me. "I'll bring Switch here! I promise. I promise you."

Wallace eyes me levelly. "We tried that, remember? Just now?"

The men behind me laugh.

"Then the Judge himself. I can get him into the open."

The laughter stops.

"No, you can't," Moira says to me, and then she turns toward Wallace. "He can't."

"I can." My mind is working feverishly, trying to think of a plan. "I know how to do it."

"How's that?" Wallace asks.

"I'll tell him about you. I'll tell him you contacted me, that you're trying to get me to turn." A distant thought occurs to me—the pieces start to fall into place.

Both groups will be brought to the same place.

"The Judge will kill you," Wallace says flatly.

"Not if I tell him we haven't met yet. Not if I tell him I went to him right away. And not if I bring him where you want to meet me."

Wallace scratches his earlobe. "You're going to double-cross him by pretending to double-cross us?"

"Yes."

Wallace stops scratching his ear and pulls his phone out of his pocket. He dials a number, watching me the entire time. "It's off," he says and hangs up.

I relax, although the arms holding me don't.

"You're a weird guy, Tom," Wallace comments. "For the second time today, you just saved the life of a woman who would kill you."

"I know."

"So you'd better hope we survive."

"I know that, too."

Wallace uses his foot to push out the chair in front of me. "Now sit down, and let's figure out exactly what you're going to tell the Judge."

ᘓᘓᘓ

I leave the restaurant twenty minutes later and head toward my truck. The sedan with the tinted windows is gone.

I reach into my pocket for my keys and hear a rushing sound behind me. Someone slams me into my truck's door before I can turn around.

The wind flies out of me and I drop to my knees. A kick lands in my ribs. It doesn't hurt, but it spins me over and I end up on the ground.

I look up at Garrett.

The polo and khakis are gone in favor of jeans and a hoodie.

"I heard what you did to my partner," he says and kicks me again.

I see the kick coming, but it still hurts when his boot crashes into my arm. "I didn't have a choice," I tell him.

He pulls out a knife.

"I didn't have a choice!" I say again urgently. "They were going to kill both of us. Now we're both alive."

He presses his knife against my neck.

Everything in my body is taut, and it's hard to keep still without trembling. I want to push myself away, to grab for his knife, to stop it from pressing into my throat. "Wallace wants me alive," I say slowly, carefully. "He needs me to get the Judge."

"You don't think I know that? I was listening the entire time. I know what you're doing, and I know you can't be trusted."

"That's not true. I'll do whatever I can to keep me and Julie safe. Even if that means double-crossing the Judge and Lucy and Switch, and working with Wallace and Moira and you."

He pauses. I can feel my skin folding over the pressed blade.

"My partner might die," Garrett says.

"Then I'm the best chance you have at getting revenge. Please."

Garrett looks at me for a long moment.

CHAPTER 56

Daniel

I've never seen Lucy this chatty, talking about her sister and the Judge and DC and everything else the way young girls do as I drive her through the most fucking hipster neighborhood ever on the way to Moira's house and it's like Lucy has a sixth sense like maybe because she's a twin and she's spent her whole life hanging with Switch and knows what she's thinking and so maybe she knows what everyone else is thinking too, but she doesn't seem to a know a thing about my thoughts as she talks about some kid named Julie and doesn't notice how little I'm talking back or that my bleared eyes haven't once looked away from the windshield and I'm glad because Lucy's on her way to die.

We pull to a stop in front of the house. Lucy pushes open her door.

"Hey," I tell her, trying to think of something to say because even though Lucy is kind of an asshole and her sister is crazy as fuck, I've never had a problem with either of them, and I'd hoped that, somehow, neither sister would get killed, even though I know my opinion sucked shit and I'd never be able to change Wallace's mind. I'd joined with the Eastmen because I wouldn't just be a driver for them but I didn't know what to expect or what would happen, and now I'm sitting in a car with Lucy outside of a house full of men waiting to murder her.

"Hey, what?" she asks back.

"Nothing, just…" And I don't know what to say and she's looking at me so I ask, "Do you have a lighter?" and she does that eye roll thing and reaches into her jacket pocket and tosses it to me.

"Brought it just for you," she says and then she also says, "Knew you'd ask," and then Lucy stares at me as I say nothing and, instead, I look down at the lighter in my lap.

Lucy leaves the car and I watch her as she heads up the small sidewalk and then the three porch steps and stands at the door and then she turns and looks at me and I stare back at her and my face must have given it away because something terrible crosses her expression and the door opens behind her and someone pulls her inside.

I stay in the car and pull out a cigarette and my hands are shaking so much I can't hold it, let alone light it, so I let it drop the floor and pop open the glove compartment and pull out a joint and stick it in my mouth and it sits there. I push open the car door and climb out and throw the joint into the street and hurry to Moira's front door.

I listen at the door, looking around to see if the neighbors or cars or anyone anywhere is around and no there's no one.

The door opens quietly and I creep inside and the living room is empty. I walk deeper in and the bedroom door is open but just a crack and I look through the crack and everything in my body suffocates.

Lucy is curled up on her side and four men stand around her and their boots drive into her and I wonder why she isn't making any sounds until I see the shine of the duct tape around the back of her shaved head and I realize they gagged her. And she *is* making sounds. I can just barely hear them, little grunts and moans and then something else, higher-pitched that I don't recognize at first. She's crying.

I stay quiet but my insides scream.

They pull her up and two of the men hold her because she's slumping, and a man stands in front of her and punches her in the face hard so hard her head snaps back and falls forward and a thin stream of blood splashes to the floor. He lifts her by the chin and does it again and then again. And then those men have to hold her up because there's nothing in her legs, her knees are collapsed.

The fourth man undoes his belt and I get even more scared because I think he's going to do something else but he doesn't do that and, instead, he stands behind her and wraps the belt around her neck and drags her down to the floor and parades her around in a circle like she's some kind of dog. Every time he comes near the door I move away because even though they wouldn't care that I'm here, they might ask me to help or watch. And I don't want Lucy to see me.

And then I see a gun on the floor near me that one of the men must have dropped.

Lucy is barely crawling, just being dragged really, and the men hit or kick or spit on her as she passes. Finally, she can't move anymore and the guy tries to drag her until it looks like her head is about to pop off or explode and then she lies on her back and the men fall on her and it's like a fog of punches and kicks and pain. I stare at the gun.

When I finally look back the men's hands have turned into knives, knives pushing into her stomach, knives like starving animals desperate to feed.

CHAPTER 57

Tom

Y ou wouldn't know that a hit squad had been about to invade my house.
Parked empty cars fill the sides of the street. People trail pets. Just an average day in Federal Hill.

I walk inside my house, lock the door behind me.

"Julie?"

No answer. Good.

"Switch?"

She walks into the hallway.

"The Eastmen made contact with me," I tell her.

For the first time, Switch seems surprised. Her eyes widen.

"A man called me when we got back this morning," I tell her, repeating what Wallace and I rehearsed. "He said he was from Dave's office, and Dave was sick and I needed to pick Julie up. When I went outside to go get her, a man was out there. He was tall with short dark hair. He said his name was Wallace."

Switch just looks at me.

"He told me he's with the Eastmen, and said he wants to meet with me later tonight. He said if I don't show up, he'll end my life, and Julie's life."

Switch still doesn't say anything.

"I don't know what to do," I lie. "But I thought I should tell you. I don't want the Judge to think I'm working with anyone but him. Do you know where Lucy is?"

She shakes her head.

"You don't know either? We need to find her. They want to meet at Fort McHenry at midnight. Can you tell the Judge for me? If this Wallace is someone important, maybe the Judge can ambush him or something. Set a trap."

Switch looks at me.

"You understand, right? Do you understand what I'm saying?"

Switch keeps looking at me. Then she pulls out her phone.

ల౨ల౨

Fort McHenry is locked at midnight, but I scale the fence pretty easily and don't see any security. That surprises me but, then again, there's not much to steal at an old battlefield.

I zip my jacket and head down the stone walkway, past a clump of petrified canyons pointing in every direction and stone embankments built into the earth, built to protect soldiers as artillery rained down. I climb a small staircase and walk a few steps onto the grass. Fort McHenry is on the banks of the Patapsco River and I can see the lights twinkling on Key Bridge in the distance. I turn and look back at the cannons and imagine men running between them, explosions deafening their ears. I always feel strange when I visit old battlefields, places where men worked and killed and cried and died. Strange to be standing in the same spot where someone's blood soaked the ground. Their blood and my body, separated by nothing but time.

If I think about it hard enough, if I let my mind drift into the past, then I can almost feel them.

Switch told me that the Judge would meet me here. I pull out my phone and check the time. Five to midnight.

Cannons are all around me. Black cannons, posed cannons, desperate cannons. And, somewhere hidden in the night, the Eastmen wait with them.

Switch called the Judge. He'll be here at midnight. The Eastmen will rush him, take him. Lucy had texted us and told us she was all right, just doing something for the Judge, and would be back later. And when she comes back, the Eastmen will move in on the twins. The Judge and his men will die tonight, in one fell swoop.

But, hopefully, they'll take out most of Wallace's men on the way out. If whoever wins is left weakened, then they won't care about me.

Besides, they both think I'm helping them.

My hands will be covered in blood, but it's the only thing I can do.

I look into the night and wonder how many of the Eastmen are out there. And I wonder if the Judge is there, watching me, waiting. About to walk toward me.

When he does, Julie and I will finally be free. Free from the danger I've brought on us, free from the violence that's engulfed me.

At least, that's how I rationalize it.

I wonder if there's a way to avoid the violence, if there's a way to bring peace to both groups. Maybe when the Judge comes out and the Eastmen rush him, I can urge them to throw down their guns, to reject senseless revenge. I see myself as a messianic figure, bringing love and harmony. And maybe not even stopping here. Maybe heading to the most troubled streets in Baltimore and urging gang leaders and drug dealers to work in unity.

I imagine myself possibly nominated for some type of prize.

Then again, I'll be lucky to live through the night, much less convince hardened killers not to murder each other.

I sit on the grass and stare out into the black water.

It doesn't seem like a smart thing to do, to turn my back on a group of killers prowling the grounds behind me but, weirdly, I'm not that scared. I wonder about the Judge, what he looks like, who he is. Odd that an unseen man can command such respect, such strict obedience. Mack had been a geriatric geezer, but there was a hardness to him that you didn't question and, besides, you knew him. The Judge is an invisible force, something beneath the surface of the water that you don't want to emerge.

I pull out my phone and check the time again.

12:10.

I send a text to Switch. *Where is he*

I wait a few minutes until my phone buzzes, and I'm so sure it's Switch that I answer without checking the screen.

"You fucker," Moira spits. "You set us up."

"Set you up?" I cover the phone, look around, and speak low. "I've been waiting here for the Judge. I did my part."

"The men who were supposed to be there are dead. Haven't you realized you're alone?"

I look around. "I thought they were really good at hiding."

"They're dead. What kind of game are you playing, Tom? What kind of shit are you trying to pull?"

"I don't know what happened!"

"Here's what happened," Moira says. "You tried to save that crazy bitch's life and ended up killing two of ours."

"I didn't do anything to help her! I gave her to you!"

"Then where is she? She wasn't at your house."

"She was supposed to be! Honestly, I didn't—"

"We told you not to double-cross us."

The line disconnects.

"I don't know what's happening!" I cry out helplessly. I call Moira back. No answer. I hurry to my feet, still expecting to see men emerge from the shadows around me, but the night stays quiet. I run back up the path, passing the cannons and mounds of cannonballs.

I reach my truck, climb inside, and everything is a blur. I start the truck and head home, dialing Moira again. She doesn't answer, so I try Switch. Nothing.

My phone buzzes.

As desperately as I've been trying to reach people, I'm suddenly afraid to answer.

I pull over to the side of the road, kill the engine, and pick up my phone.

It's not a phone call. It's a message.

I click and see a video with a short title.

From Wallace

I play it.

The video is dark and grainy until I finally make out a door. I study the video intensely, holding the phone close to my face. The door looks familiar, but I can't figure out where I've seen it until the door opens.

Ruth.

She stands there, the light from the inside of her house illuminating her, and her face is a kaleidoscope of changing emotions, curiosity to confusion to fear.

And then I see a gun rise.

I hear a shot.

I watch her fall.

CHAPTER 58

Switch

I stop the big van behind Teacher Tom's truck and see the back of Teacher Tom's head in his driver's seat. I walk over to the passenger side and climb inside. He's holding his phone in his hand and I take it and look at it and hope its Lucy but it's not. I watch a video of a sort of pretty lady getting shot in the face.

"I called Dave, and he was on the way to the hospital," Teacher Tom tells me, and he's very quiet when he speaks. "They don't know what's going to happen. She's not dead yet."

He sounds like he wants to say more, but doesn't.

"You can't go to the hospital," I tell him, and I'm proud of myself because it's something Lucy would have thought of. "The Eastmen will be there."

He just looks at me with sad face.

"Excuse me," I say, and I step outside.

I call the Judge. No answer.

I call Driver Daniel. No answer.

I call lots of people and no answers.

I chew my thumbnail for a moment and my phone buzzes.

Driver Daniel calling me back.

"Switch!" Driver Daniel says. "I can't get hold of anyone! It's the Eastmen. They're going after all of us."

Driver Daniel sounds scared, scared.

"You seen the Judge?" I ask.

"I don't know where he is," Driver Daniel says. "Just tell me where you are, so I can come find you. Please. We have to stick together."

Something in his voice makes me give the phone a hard look.

"How do they know where we live?" I ask, and then I think of something. "You know where we live, Driver Daniel."

Driver Daniel is quiet, and I start jumping up and down.

"Be seeing you soon, Switch," Driver Daniel says. "So will your sister."

He hangs up and I stop jumping and chew my thumbnail some more and a silly thought occurs to me. Driver Daniel doesn't know where everyone lives. So it can't just be Driver Daniel.

And then another silly thought occurs to me. It's a good thing no one was at Teacher Tom's house, because Driver Daniel definitely would have taken the Eastmen there.

And I wonder where Lucy is.

I climb back inside the truck.

Teacher Tom is still sitting there, staring forward.

"Come on," I say. "We have to go."

Nothing.

I think about slapping him like they do on TV, but I just shake his shoulder. "Come on. We have to go."

Nothing, nothing.

"I need to get Julie."

Now Teacher Tom says something. "Where are you going to take her?"

"Lucy has a secret place. No one knows about it, not even the Judge. She told me to go there if things are bad."

He shakes his head. "I'll get her."

I tell him no and he argues, but I tell him we don't have time and he argues some more and I tell him he's going to slow me down and he says I don't care and I say he'll get us all killed and he says I don't care I only care about Little Girl Julie and I wonder where Lucy is and I say very slowly I can't take you and he says I'm not asking and I feel like giggling but then I think about Little Girl Julie and I say I'm going and he says I am too and I'm all fuck this.

"Okay," I say. "But we have to go somewhere first."

"Where?"

"Your house. I forgot my pills."

"How'd you forget them?"

"Because Lucy reminds me."

Teacher Tom looks mad. "We'll get them later. We need to get my daughter!"

So we argue some more and then Teacher Tom is all: "Fine! We'll get your stupid pills. Just make it quick."

Teacher Tom drives us to his house and I tell him to go around the corner. I don't like his front door, especially since the Eastmen are hunting us. He parks and I leave him in the truck after he angry-whispers, "*Hurry!*" I skip behind the row houses then climb Teacher Tom's back fence and drop down to the other side. I don't trust the back door either, but there's a window I can climb up to and I do. It's Little Girl Julie's window, and it's unlocked, and I open it and slide in.

Bananas comes hopping up. I pick him up and kiss

his face and nibble his floppy flop-flop ears and then set him down in his pen.

Then I pull out my knife.

I open Little Girl Julie's bedroom door and peek into the hallway. No one is there so I slip out. I pad down the hall to my room and find my silly pills. I take them, leave my room, and head to the dark stairs.

I see a shadow at the bottom of the stairs, and I step down a few steps—quiet, quiet, quiet—and see a man sitting there, a big gun over both his knees, facing the door. So it's a good thing I didn't go through the front door. I think about it and feel a giggle rise up my throat and I bite down on the side of my hand so I don't make a sound. But it's hard to be that quiet and I go back upstairs to the bathroom and close the door behind me and put my mouth in my elbow and laugh to myself.

The light in the hallway comes on.

I try to remember if Lucy ever told me what to do if I was trapped in a bathroom, but I can't think of anything. I hear the footsteps getting closer, closer. Finally I pull the shower curtain closed as fast as I can.

The door is thrown open and I see the big gun, and then a little man behind it. He uses one hand to pull the curtain away.

I step out from behind the door and let the Little Man turn toward me. I shove the knife right under his chin with one hand and take his gun away with the other. Little Man tries to say something but can't, and then I lay him down in the shower. I pull his neck open to make sure he's dead and then I lay his gun next to him and go outside.

I creep down the stairs and into the den. A man is sitting in the chair Teacher Tom likes to sit in and he tries to jump up when I walk in. But I push him down and hold my knife to his chest. He looks very scared but also very sad.

"Look," Sad Man says, "I don't know who you are, but I'm with the FBI. My name is Garrett. Agent Garrett. Can I show you my badge?"

He looks at me very carefully and reaches into his pocket and slowly pulls out a little wallet with a shiny badge.

"Do you see?" Sad Man asks.

I step toward him. "I dunno."

Sad Man looks scared and raises an arm. "I'm sorry about your sister. It wasn't me."

That stops me. "Where's Lucy?"

He tells me.

I check the rest of the house after and look for other people, but they were the only ones here. I wipe the Sad Man's blood off my face with a towel and change my shirt.

Teacher Tom won't be happy about all the blood everywhere. But Judge will clean it up. Judge doesn't forget.

Oh, my pill.

I swallow a pill, burp, and go back to the truck.

CHAPTER 59

Daniel

I take out a joint as I sit in my car and nervously wait for Vince and his partner whose name I haven't been told yet to come back and, all things considered, it's a good idea I didn't bring any white shit with me because I'm already completely on fucking edge and scared. I feel like I'm trying to keep my balance on a razor over a pit of fire. So yeah probably good that I'm not letting coke tense me up even if I could use the confidence.

I suck in the joint, hold it, let it out.

I don't know if drugs will affect me tonight or if my mind is too distracted disjointed distant to be affected. I thought I was going to die from fear when we pulled up here and Vince's partner asked if we were all ready to go inside and I sat in my seat and stared forward and was about to say, "I'm just a driver" and I heard Vince say "leave him here in case we need to drive off fast" and his partner grunted and they grabbed masks and headed into the apartment building.

I ash the joint out the window and my muscles tense

and I think about the house that went bad and I think maybe I shouldn't sit here in this car, maybe I should stand in a dark corner near the apartment building, and that seems like a really good idea but then Vince and his partner come back and climb inside.

"Drive," Vince says.

I do and don't go anywhere in particular. I take a lot of back roads and sharp cuts and make sure no one can follow us, and I listen to Vince and his partner talk about how the man they just killed had tried to run and force his window open but they just grabbed him and gutted him and I know his name, but oh God, I can't say his name.

Some days I could give a shit about the dead and sometimes they rock me and I'm not sure but I'm pretty sure it's because of the drugs.

Like, with Lucy.

I didn't even like her and her sister just embarrassed me on the phone but there was just so much to it like the violence of how it was done and the walls of Moira's house when I went back to help clean up and more than anything how this had even happened at Moira's home, where I stood a day before and she stood and acted as if a woman wouldn't be slaughtered on the floor the next day. Something about that made me feel so...so...so...so...

So lonely, that's what it was, and I'd gone to the bathroom and turned on the fan and the water to drown out any sounds I made and cried helplessly.

A light from the back of the car. I looked through the rearview mirror and see Vince check his phone.

"That's all of them," he says, and puts a hand on my shoulder, "good job on those addresses."

"We got all of them?" Vince's partner asks.

No sound for a moment. "Not the Judge," Vince says. "And they don't know where Switch is. And we haven't heard from Garrett. One house went wrong. They

killed..." and I scream inside so I won't hear Vince say
the name of this man who trusted me, "...but someone
else must have been there. Wallace headed over there and
found two bodies, ours and theirs. Moira figures that
teacher double-crossed us, told the retarded twin what
was happening."

And I don't say anything but I know it must have
been the Judge escaping.

We're all silent for a bit as I think about all the death
and how it's gotten to be too much and how now that
everything's over I'm just going to drive away from Baltimore tomorrow, away from everyone and everything
I've ever known because for some weird reason I feel like
I've discovered a traitor and I'm angry and not scared,
although that might be because the Judge's men are all
dead.

There's something in me resolute, determined.

I will leave this life, this haze of violence and fear
that I'm buried in like a fog that's rolled over and won't
lift. I'll leave it all. What has been done can be forgiven,
absolved, repented, if never undone. Even if never undone, I am a good man. I did not kill, will not kill.

Another light from the back. "Looks like they found
Switch," Vince says.

CHAPTER 60

Julie

I'm just about to undo my bra for Anthony because I can tell he's getting frustrated with the latch.

"Stop fucking, you guys," Jenny says. "I think my dad is coming down."

Anthony freezes beneath me, and I lift the covers and peer out. Jenny's watching TV at the foot of the bed.

"He is?" I ask.

She turns around and looks at me. "I just heard him. Shit, you need to fix your hair."

I climb out of the covers, pull on my shirt, buckle my pants, and Jenny hands me a brush to run through my hair. Anthony sits up, reaches for his shirt with his long arm, and pulls it on. He looks toward the basement window. "Should I hide outside?"

Footsteps coming. "Jenny? Honey?"

"I'll wait outside," Anthony decides, and he stands on the bed, pushes open the window, letting in cold air, and climbs outside. I'm too busy making sure I look presentable to pay attention to him, but I tell him to wait a moment and climb on the bed to kiss him. We kiss, and then he disappears.

I close the window after him, hop on the floor, and Jenny looks around to make sure everything is okay. I nod and she unlocks and opens her bedroom door.

"Hi, honey," her dad says, and he looks at me and his eyes travel down and I realize my shirt is too low. I self-consciously adjust it and he looks back up. "Julie, your dad is here? He said he needs to pick you up?"

"Really?" I frown and follow him upstairs, glancing back at Jenny and the window.

My dad is standing in the hall looking nervous as hell.

"We have to get going," he says.

A sinking feeling. "Is everything okay?"

"Ruth is in the hospital," he tells me.

"Aunt Ruth?" For some reason, my hand is at my neck. "What happened? Did Uncle Dave find out?"

Dad looks confused for a moment. "No."

"Do you know if she's okay?"

"She was, she was involved in a mugging. I don't know."

"What?"

"Hon, we have to go."

"Okay, let me get my stuff." I run downstairs, back to the bedroom. Jenny is still there and Anthony is with her. They're sitting on the floor.

"Jesus, fuck," I tell them. "You're just sitting here with the goddamn door open? What would have happened if your dad came back?"

"It's not like he's that quiet on the stairs," Anthony says. "I'd be out that window in a second. Or just let him see me here." He shrugs. "What's he going to do?"

Jenny laughs. "You're such a fucking tough guy, right?"

"You don't think I am?"

"I think we have a total of three pussies in this room," Jenny says, and she looks at me. "What's wrong?"

"My aunt got hurt. She's in the hospital."

"O-M-G," Jenny says. "Is she going to be okay?"

"I don't know. Going to find out now."

"Call me when you have news," Anthony tells me.

I nod and give him a deep kiss, let our tongues wrestle for a few moments. "Tomorrow."

I head upstairs and ignore Jenny's perv dad. My dad opens the door, looks around like he's some kind of escaped convict, and we walk out.

"What hospital?" I ask him.

"I'm taking you somewhere else."

I look at him sharply. "Why?"

"It's—" My dad stops and looks at me.

"What?" I ask.

"I need you to do me a favor," he says. "I need you to do what I tell you tonight, and not ask any questions. Some of Switch and Lucy's friends showed up at the house, and I need you to stay somewhere else. The twins won't be with us tomorrow. Looks like you were right. Not a good idea to let them stay with us."

My dad's truck pulls up. Switch is driving.

"Probably not a good idea to let the coked-out one drive your truck," I tell him.

He looks and grimaces.

"Dad, it's okay." I give him this one, since he's so stressed. "I'll do what you say."

We get in the truck and drive in silence. Seems like forever.

I wonder if Ruth is okay. I hope so. It was terrible

when my mom died, even if I was really young when it happened. Nothing much has happened since. Life seems that way, for the most part. You grow up and go to work and occasionally fuck your spouse. No wonder people like Ruth have affairs. You probably get so bored when you're old.

I understand that, but don't really get it. That's probably because I've found someone to love. If you have that, then you understand what happiness really is, and how unbreakable it is, because it's founded in love.

I wrote that for a poem a week ago. It was really good. Deep. I got an A-minus.

We finally arrive at a crappy little apartment building. I have no idea where we are, except for somewhere outside of Baltimore. My dad doesn't look happy about being here either.

The apartment is on the ground floor and small inside. It smells dirty, like it hasn't been washed for weeks.

"Lucy lives here?" he asks.

"Not anymore," Switch says.

I walk into the room and think this is a good place to be alone, because no one else would ever want to come here.

"We need to go," Switch says.

"Do you have anything to eat?" my dad asks her.

"We need to go."

"So," he says, "that's a no?"

"Dad, it's okay," I say. "I'll be okay."

He hugs me tight, tells me he loves me, and then he's gone.

CHAPTER 61

Tom

A re you one thousand percent sure no one knows about that place?" I ask Switch as we drive off.
"Just me and Lucy."

"And where's Lucy? Have you heard from her yet?"

"The Eastmen, they killed her."

I start. "Lucy's dead?"

Switch nods.

My mind feels like it's fallen and landed on a rock. Switch glances over at me.

"Are you sure?"

She nods. Her eyes are blank, her face innocent, as if she can break into a smile at a moment's notice.

"Can you pull over?"

"Okay."

Now there's no choice. I have to end it. I have to do whatever I can. The Eastmen are going to win this war, and I have to make sure Julie and I will be safe.

So there's only one thing I can do.

"I'm going to call Moira," I tell Switch.

"Moira won't meet you," Switch says, as she steers my truck over to the side of the road.

"She'll meet me," I pull out my gun and point it at her, "because I'm giving her you."

CHAPTER 62

Moira answers before the first ring ends.

"Tom?" she asks.

"Is Lucy dead?"

"Yes."

I rub my eyes.

"I have Switch," I tell her.

"What do you mean, you have Switch?"

"I'm through with this. I'm through with all of it. I have a gun pointed at her right now."

Switch looks unhappily at the gun I have pointed at her. We're standing outside of my truck, on the side of some dark road. The light from my open cab illuminates us.

"So you're just going to hand her over to us?" Moira asks.

"That's right. I want me and Julie out of this."

Muffled voices. "Why should we trust you?" Moira asks.

"I have nothing to threaten you with. All I'm doing is giving Switch to you for our freedom. This is the only thing I can do. You know that."

"Huh." She doesn't sound convinced.

"So where do I meet you?"

"We'll pick the place," Moira says. "Somewhere outside the city." I hear muffled voices again. "The bridge in Lock Raven Reservoir. Half an hour."

☙☙☙

"Take out your knife and drop it," I tell Switch.

She does.

"Kick it over to me."

The knife slides near my foot. I quickly pick it up and tuck it into my pocket.

"Now give me your phone."

Switch reaches into her pocket and pulls it out.

"Toss it to me. Gently."

She does.

I catch it with one hand, keeping my gun on Switch with the other. "You said you called the Judge. Is his number in here?"

Switch shakes her head.

"Tell me the number. I know you know it. I want him there too."

She does.

☙☙☙

Sitting in the passenger seat of my own truck is a bit disorienting but, with Switch driving, I finally have a moment to think. "This is my fault," I say to Switch, and myself. "I never should have let you or them control me. All of you put me into this situation. I should have told you to fuck off."

Switch doesn't say anything.

"And you all always try and tell me I brought this on myself, back when I first went to Mack. That was a mistake, but I'm not paying for that mistake for the rest of my life. That's how you sick fucks control me, and control each other. You act like everything someone does is a long string of consequences, so you can excuse yourselves from the horrible shit you do. Like when Diane told me that she and Bardos were just the bullets of the gun that everyone fires."

Switch stays silent.

"I believed her a little," I continue. "I believed her, but now Ruth may be dead, and I want to blame myself, to hate myself, to believe my actions led to her death and it's all my fault. But I loved her. You people shot her. You people..."

Switch slows the car, pulls over to the side of the road.

"You did this," I whisper. "All of you did this."

Switch stops the car and kills the ignition.

"Lucy's dead," she says.

"I know."

"I don't know what to do."

I think about Ruth and tighten my grip around the gun. "Just keep driving."

CHAPTER 63

We slowly drive down a long dark narrow road blanketed by trees. After nearly thirty minutes, a car's headlights flash to our left. I pull into a deep inlet on the side.

Four cars are waiting for us. A fifth pulls up behind my truck, trapping us in a circle.

I turn off the ignition. Switch looks at me one last time.

"Get out."

Headlights light up as we step outside. I see shadows of tall trees around us and, beyond them, the slopes of high hills. I've been here once before, years ago, when Renee wanted to visit different bridges in Maryland.

A man steps into the circle with us, a gun in his hand. Others join him, maybe six or seven more.

"Gun on the ground," one of the men says. I oblige him.

Wallace steps in, his long lean body lit by the lights. He looks at me and Switch and smiles a little. All of the headlights except for one extinguish.

"Finally brought her to me?" he asks.

"You can have her. Just leave me and my family alone."

The smile stays. "You know, Tom, it's—" Wallace looks at me closely. "Have you been crying, because of what happened tonight?"

"Yes."

The men laugh.

After they're done laughing, I ask, "Are we done now? Do we have a deal?"

"Nah."

"But you told me we would."

More laughs.

I turn to Switch. "You've ruined my life," I tell her. "You and your people and everyone."

Switch has her eyes closed and is muttering to herself.

"I should have just killed you myself, left your body for them to find." I grab her neck with one hand. Her eyes pop open and she takes a step back.

"Easy, Tom," Wallace warns me.

"Why won't you let me out?" I shout.

I push into Switch and we fall to the ground. She grunts underneath me and, like a snake, slips to the side. I try to grab her hair but there isn't any so I grab her chin, my fingers in her mouth, and push the back of her head into the ground. I hear more laughter from the men. Switch grunts again and I bury my mouth next to her ear.

"Take the knife," I whisper. "Run down the road to the bridge."

I worry she didn't hear me, but Switch reaches for the knife and pulls it free. I feel a burning rush over my arm, like heat from dry ice. I cry out and fall back and push myself away from her. Blood runs down my fingers.

Switch springs to her feet and races to the closest car. The sudden deafening sound of a shot rings out, more shots, and I stay as low to the ground as possible and watch Switch jump on the hood of the car and then the roof and then, as gracefully as a cat, leap off and disappear into the night.

"Shit!" Wallace curses, and his men run past me, following her. I stay on the ground and pick myself up shakily, holding my wounded arm with one hand. Wallace stops next to me.

"You're with us," he says. "Come on."

"I'll go with you," Moira joins in.

I hadn't seen her earlier. She must have been waiting in one of the cars. The three of us follow Switch and Wallace's men into the woods.

I hear them ahead of us, crashing through branches, and I see lights in the distance. Wallace runs next to me, muttering to himself. Moira is somewhere behind. The pain from my arm reverberates through my body with each hard step.

"There!" Wallace cries, and Switch's small body is running on the road toward the Loch Raven Reservoir Bridge. The bridge is made up old steel and covered with an arch of beams. We reach the edge of the bridge and run onto it, our steps echoing. Switch is at the other end and a couple of the men shoot at her, but their bullets miss. She stops and turns toward us.

That's when I know he's here.

The Judge hadn't said a word on the phone, but he had listened, and he had done what I said.

I turn and the biggest man I've ever seen is holding the biggest gun I've ever seen, like a cannon posed on the side of a mountain. The man is so large that I'm almost too shocked to do anything, but there's an explosion behind me, thunder splitting open hell. The reverberation throws me forward.

The wind is knocked out of me and I can't hear anything when I land except for a low whistle. I crawl on my hands and knees and look up. The man's gun glows. And then the whistle slows and separates into gunfire.

The men behind me scream.

The gun suddenly stops. I look up and the giant man tosses it to the ground. Then looks in my direction and reaches down. I worry he's going to grab me, but instead he pulls Moira up by her neck.

She screams, kicks at him, tries to push his face away. I watch, transfixed. He probably tips the scale at over three-hundred pounds and is well over six feet tall. He's bald and white and wears jeans and a zipped leather jacket.

"Please," Moira says. "Please, don't kill me. Please."

He cuts off her voice with a twist of his hands and lets her lifeless body drop to the ground.

There's a gunshot and the man's shoulder snaps back. I look next to me and see Wallace lying on his stomach, holding a gun. He lifts it to fire again and a knife swoops down, stabbing his hand. He cries out and the gun drops.

Switch. She reaches down, takes the gun, and steps away.

"Teacher Tom," she says. "This is the Judge."

The Judge takes off his jacket and examines his dark bulletproof vest. Then he walks past us, over to the men sprawled on the ground. He examines them carefully, picking up their guns and throwing them over the side of the bridge and into the water. Then he grabs two of the men and drags them over to us. These men are still alive, but barely. I can hear one's watery breaths, see the other's right foot twitch. The Judge leaves them, walks over to the side of the bridge, and comes back with a coil of rope.

"Teacher Tom can go, right?" Switch asks.

The Judge looks at me for a long moment. He nods.

I head back to the woods and my truck. My arm still hurts, but the pain is numbed. I walk back to my truck and I'm about to climb inside, but stop.

I turn and head back to the bridge. I stay in the trees and watch as Switch and the Judge tie a noose around each man's neck and throw them over the side.

Ten bodies dangle when it's over.

CHAPTER 64

*B*ALTIMORE, MD.. Police reported that a man walking his dog saw ten men hanging off the side of the Loch Raven Reservoir Bridge early this morning. The victims, most of whom had been shot prior to being hung, have not been identified, and the motives behind the execution-styled killing remain unclear. Several possibilities were suggested by journalists to the spokesperson for the police department, including Mexican cartel-styled violence, or the fighting between city gangs spreading further out into the county, neither of which have been confirmed as of this report.

BALTIMORE, MD. A local woman was shot in the doorway of her Homeland residence late last night. She is expected to survive. Authorities have no suspects.

❧❧❧

I push open the door to Ruth's hospital room. She's lying down, a bandage covering the left half of her face.

Dave sits next to her, her small hand in his two giant ones.

"Can I come in?" Neither of them respond. "How's she doing? Is she awake yet?"

"I'm awake," Ruth says, her voice low, hoarse.

I walk around the bed and sit in a chair next to Dave. From this side, you can see glimpses of lumped flesh and blood underneath Ruth's bandage.

"She's going to lose her eye," Dave tells me.

I can't breathe for a minute. "Really?"

"And maybe some hearing," Ruth says.

"Oh."

I watch her hand tremble.

"Is there nerve damage?" I ask.

Ruth raises her hand. The shaking doesn't stop. "This is because I keep remembering it."

I look away and rub the bandage on my arm.

I feel awful.

Seeing Ruth here is unreal, and then it's entirely too real, the kind of pain so sudden it hits like a bad dream, leaves you sweating and gasping as you sit up in confusion.

And sadness, sadness that seems to cover me the way a sheet covers a corpse, as if it will lie there eternally, and it will. It's guilt but more than guilt. Despair. Despair for what I've caused.

"I don't even know what he wanted," Ruth asks. "He didn't take anything."

Dave shakes his head. "Probably something against white people. Or wealthy people. This city is falling apart."

"You don't know if they were white or black," Ruth says. "The man was wearing a mask, and his whole body was covered."

Dave grunts.

A knock on the door. A head pokes through.

Switch.

"Oops," she says. She backs out and closes the door.

"No problem," Dave calls out.

"I'm going to use the bathroom," I tell them and step outside. Switch is standing across the hall. A few nurses are gathered at the far end. Otherwise, it's empty. I walk over to her.

"Everything's clean and I brought Julie back," Switch says. "And I got my stuff."

"Good."

She looks around. "This is the second hospital I've been in today."

It takes me a moment. "You visited Peterson?"

She nods.

I'm not sure what to say.

"Are you okay?" I ask. "Without Lucy?"

"I dunno."

I look at her closely, trying to see if there is any emotion in her wide brown eyes. Sadness. Fear.

Nothing.

"Do you miss her?" I ask.

Switch looks right, looks left, and leans in close. "I don't know what to do," she whispers.

"You can—" I start and then stop, horrified that I'd been about to invite Switch to live with me and Julie. The idea had been so natural that my response almost slipped out.

She does need a place to live, and someone to help her, and…okay, Switch needs a lot more than that. And there isn't anything I can offer her.

"What?" Switch asks. "You said *you can*."

"You can do anything you set your mind to," I suggest.

"Okay," Switch says. She looks down the hall, to the exit.

"Where are you going to go?" I ask.

"To Lucy's apartment." She starts to walk away.

"Hey, Switch."

She turns and looks back toward me.

"Tell him I'm out."

She nods.

"Stay safe," I add.

Switch smiles. "Lucy used to tell me that."

We look at each other for a few more moments, and her smile fades, and something dark crosses her face. And then she's gone.

I return to the room, sit back down next to Dave.

"Are you in any pain?" I ask Ruth.

She nods. "More scared about losing my sight, even if it's just in one eye."

"I'm here for you," Dave says, and he lifts her hand and kisses it. "I promise."

"I'm glad," Ruth tells him, her hands in his, her eye on me. "I need that now. More than anything."

Tragedy binds them.

Despite the guilt I feel when I look at Ruth's bandaged eye, the guilt hanging over me like a fist about to smash down, sadness fills me. I look down, then back up and into Ruth's good eye. Ruth blinks and turns away, turns her head toward Dave.

დილო

Dave steps out of Ruth's room when I do.

"Tom. You have a minute?"

"Yeah."

"How's Julie?" he asks.

"She's okay. I'll bring her by later. I wanted to see Ruth before she did."

"Good idea."

We don't say anything for a moment.

"I know you were sleeping with her," Dave says.

More silence.

"I'm sorry," I tell him.

"Don't say you're sorry," he replies. "You wouldn't have done it if you were sorry."

"She didn't want to hurt you."

"She wouldn't have done it if she didn't want to hurt me."

Points I can't argue.

"The truth is," Dave continues, "it's probably good she got that love from somebody. I wasn't giving it to her. Ruth and I had problems. And, for the longest time, I knew something was happening with the two of you, and I didn't say anything. And even though I want to care, even though I want to say I cared, if I had really cared, I would have said something."

"Listen," I tell him, choosing my words carefully, "you're being too logical. You're trying to explain emotions. The truth is, Ruth regretted it. So did I. But we couldn't stop."

"Tom," Dave says. "Are you trying to get me to kick your ass?"

"I don't know what I'm doing."

"You're telling me I don't understand emotions," Dave says, his voice thick. He wipes his hand over his eyes again. "But the truth is, I don't understand you."

"You don't?"

"I know you don't feel bad about what you did. Ever since Renee died, you've acted like the world owes you something, like you're not accountable for your actions.

You pawn Julie off on us when you're busy without giving a shit about her, you slept with Ruth without caring what it would do to us, you don't care about anyone but yourself. And you've been secretive lately, like you're smoking too much pot or drinking too much, and you probably are. Everything you're doing is wrong, and you don't care. I'll never understand that, never understand how a man can raise a daughter and not strive to be a better person. Not even *want* to be. You're a shitty human being."

I remember the Eastmen, their bodies hanging from the bridge.

"But here's the thing," Dave says, his voice hoarse. "You gave Ruth love, and she sure as hell didn't have it from me. And if there's one thing I can give my wife today and from now on, it's that. So stay the hell away from her. I learned my lesson. Learn yours."

I don't say anything as he goes back to her.

ℰ�⋐

"*That* was a violent-ass book," Simon says. "I loved it!"

The class laughs.

"Glad you liked it," I tell him. "Remember that your papers are due next week."

"Seriously," Simon goes on, enthused, "that guy ended up with his head on the side of a horse. That's some Fallujah shit there."

"Thanks for the input. See you all next week."

The students start to pack up and file out.

"Simon," I ask. "Can you stay for a couple of minutes?"

He approaches my desk as the last students leave.

"I can't have you coming back," I tell him. "The university has a policy against non-registered students attending classes."

"Oh," he says, disappointed. "I checked. It's too late to sign up."

"You can always take this class next semester. If it's offered."

"Shit," he tells me. "I really liked reading this book. I don't read a lot."

I don't care much for Simon, but that touches something in me.

"You really liked it?" I ask. "Especially the violent parts, I take it."

He smiles sheepishly. "I guess. Yeah, those parts stuck out. You know, I was reading about this Hemingway guy online, and someone was saying how he was able to get to, like, what being human is all about. Like, his writing related to everyone."

"I see."

"It's not like I've seen a lot of violence, or been in the military or a cop or anything. But something about it, I don't know, connected. Reading parts of this felt like firing a gun. I go to the range when I get pissed off, and it feels good."

"I understand."

"You sure I can't keep coming to this class?" Simon asks, and desperation creeps into his voice. "I won't tell anyone, or speak up. I'll let other people get more involved. I promise."

It's a nice and honest sentiment.

"I have to follow the rules," I tell him.

CHAPTER 65

Switch

I walk inside and close the door behind me.

"Any word on the Eastmen?" the Judge asks me.

"I dunno."

"Come here. Stand closer to me."

I do what he tells me because Lucy once said, "If I'm ever gone, don't disobey the Judge. Promise me. Switch, promise me. You can't cross him."

"Why'd you let Ruth Wilson live?"

"I missed," I lie.

The Judge touches my wrist with his giant white hand. "Why did you let her live?" he asks me.

No, I don't like being scared. "Lucy told me not to ever do anything to hurt Julie," I tell him. "And Julie likes Ruth Wilson."

Judge stares at me and I stare back, then I think maybe I'll stare at the floor instead. "We need more men," Judge says. "Need them young, too. The way Mack used to get them. Young, make sure they're loyal. And we have some loose ends that need to be cut."

I think about loose ends that need to be cut. And that makes me think of split ends. And I think I should do something about my split ends. Then I remember I don't have any hair.

Judge is saying something. He finishes speaking and looks at me.

"You want me to?" I ask. I wasn't listening but I can find out what he wants later.

"Not yet," he says. "Soon."

"Okay."

Judge puts his hands on his thighs, leans forward. "We're your family now, Switch. Now that Lucy's gone, we're all you have. Do you understand what I'm saying, and what I mean by loose ends?"

"Yes." And I think about what Lucy said. *'Don't disobey.'*

"You want me to kill Tom?" I ask.

Judge leans back.

"His daughter knows a lot about you too," he tells me.

"You want me to kill her too?"

"Not yet," Judge says. "Soon."

CHAPTER 66

Tom

Baltimore at midnight.

I look out from my perch on the top floor of City Hospital's parking garage. Cars rush beneath me, red taillights following yellow headlights, like demons rushing after angels.

A week has passed since the Eastmen were murdered.

'*It's been a long time*,' Renee's ghost says, as she settles next to me on the ledge.

"Three years."

'*You miss me?*'

I nod.

Renee peers over the edge, onto the concrete far below. '*Are you trying to get the courage to push yourself off?*'

"I'm not going to do that to Julie."

'*Good.*'

"Renee, I've been so lost ever since you died. I'm not myself anymore."

'*You were going to change anyway, Tom. You wouldn't have been the same person six years later, no matter what happened to me.*'

"I don't like this new person. I saw those men die, and I don't feel anything. Nothing. I'm becoming like them, like Diane and Mack. I've done things I can never go back on. I'm a liar, a sinner, a murderer, an adulterer. Jesus Christ."

'*You're not Jesus Christ.*'

"I didn't mean it that way."

'*I'm kidding.*' I feel her arm on my shoulder. '*You've made some shitty decisions,*' Renee continues. '*And you're right. You are all those things, and you will be all those things. That won't change.*'

"Sounds like you're saying I should push myself off this ledge."

'*You didn't let me finish,*' Renee says. '*You've made your path hard, no question. You've done evil things, but you don't have to be an evil man. I don't think you understand that.*'

"I just feel helpless, like I don't know where I'm going, what I'm doing, what's happening. I feel unmoored."

෨෴෨

"Can I come in?"

"Hey, Dad," Julie says, sitting on her bed, a book open in front of her.

Bananas sits next to her feet, loudly eating a large carrot.

"How are you doing?"

"Okay."

"Are you sure? You're reading."

"Yeah, so?"

"You only read when you're sad."

Julie looks up at me now and smiles a little. "That's not true." Then her brow furrows. "Is it?"

I sit next to her. "What's going on? Is it about your aunt?"

"I was really scared for her," Julie admits. "And I feel terrible for her. It must be awful to lose your eyesight. Even if it's just one eye."

Guilt shakes me, like a panicked bird fluttering its wings. "We'll do whatever we can for her."

Julie nods.

"Anything else you want to talk about?" I ask.

"No."

I stand and start to walk out.

"Anthony broke up with me."

That stops me. "When?"

"A day or so ago. I didn't want to say anything while everybody was so upset."

I sit back down. "Are you okay?"

Julie looks away. "I've been crying a lot. I don't even know why it happened. I thought he was happy."

"He didn't say anything about why he did it?"

Julie shakes her head. I see tears fall and her shoulders hunch and shake. I suddenly hate Anthony. The hate burns, makes the world bleed.

I try to control myself, to push the emotion down. I put my arm around my daughter and she leans into me.

"Tara told me that he's already sleeping with someone else," Julie goes on. "I can't believe he's already with another girl."

"Someone else?" I ask. "You've had sex?"

Julie uses her shirt to wipe her eyes. "Yeah."

I stand so quickly that Bananas dives off the bed and into his pen. He races into his box and a solid *thump* comes from inside.

"You had sex? You're fifteen!"

"We used protection. It's not like I'm pregnant or anything."

"You promised you'd talk about this with me before you did anything."

"Dad! I don't want to talk about sex right now!"

As angry as I am, Julie looks so small and sad that I shelve the discussion until later.

"I feel so selfish," she says, "thinking about this with everything that happened to Aunt Ruth, but I can't help being sad."

"I know," I tell her. "But you always have me. You'll always have love. You're never alone, no matter what stupid things you do."

Julie cries, and I hold her.

"I wish," she says, into my shoulder, "I saw her more than I did."

"Ruth?"

She shakes her head. "Mom."

My arm stiffens.

"What do you mean?"

"I see her sometimes," Julie says. "She comes to me at night. I used to get scared, I used to hide under the covers and I'd look out and see her standing next to my bed."

"Really?"

"She still comes, Dad, and I don't know why. I don't know what she wants. And I think about her leaving, and I don't want to go through life alone. I miss Anthony and her and I don't want anyone else to leave."

You'll never be alone, I want to tell her.

Instead I say, "I see her too."

"You do?"

"I used to see her all the time, but it was never scary. It was nice. We'd have these weird conversations."

A little smile slips out from Julie's tears. "She was always weird."

We lapse into silence, but it's a warm silence. Outside, a car rushes past our house. I walk to the window and peer through the blinds. Night is coming, and the sky holds the promise of snow.

Years ago, Renee was here with us, in this city, in this room. And suddenly I'm amazed at how close that is, that I stand here and the only thing separating us is time. It's nothing, it's everything, it's heartbreaking to be so close to going back to what I had, who I was.

"You've really seen her?" Julie asks. "You're not just telling me that?"

"I've never told anyone. I didn't want people to think I was crazy." I pause. "I know she's not real, but it's nice."

"I know," Julie says, as I look out the window. "I want to believe."

The End

About the Author

E. A. Aymar is a monthly columnist for the *Washington Independent Review of Books*, and his fiction and nonfiction have appeared in a number of respected publications. He is a member of the Mystery Writers of America, SinC, and the International Thriller Writers, and also serves as the social media chair for the debut class of that latter organization. His debut thriller, *I'LL SLEEP WHEN YOU'RE DEAD*, was published by Black Opal Books in 2013. He lives with his family outside of Washington, DC.

CPSIA information can be obtained at www.ICGtesting.com
Printed in the USA
LVOW10s0721191215

467209LV00016B/579/P